GHOST STORIES

MEDIUM AT LARGE SHORT STORIES

MEREDITH SPIES

TRIGGER AND CONTENT WARNINGS

Please exercise care when reading if any of the following are triggers for you:

Death by violence, descriptions of murder, mentions of dead bodies, mentions of suicide, frank discussion of death and dying, emotional neglect of a child, queerphobia, discussion of terminal illness, surgery, near-death experiences, medical trauma.

Editing: Cate Ryan

Cover and Promotional Art: Samantha Santana

A FRIEND IN NEED

$\mathcal{D}$aylight sparked off the dirt road, catching minute flecks of mica left from when the sand used to be rocks, when the county tried to lay down gravel, when people gave two damns about the ass-end of Corley Road. I didn't mind it so much, being forgotten in the back end of nowhere. It was quiet, and the people I needed to see knew where I was. Hell, some of the people I didn't need to see knew where I was, too. Like the two men poking around in Sam Jenkins' old barn.

"Hey! Hey!" I tromped across the uneven ground towards the half-collapsed building. Twenty years ago, it'd still been sturdy enough for folks in the area to store shit in if the weather got too bad. Jenkins' farm had been the highest point for about four miles 'round. Now, it was a heap of rotten wood and rusted metal; what was left of the outside walls pretty much held together by termites making a concerted effort.

One of the men, on the shorter side and dressed like some sort of old painting, raised a hand to acknowledge me as I tripped and stomped over the field that'd once grown row after row of corn.

After Sam died, the farm wasn't long behind.

The land between our two barns had been our playground as boys, then as we grew, became our pride, our shared joy.

Tall and cool stalks of corn stretched over our heads, shading us when we'd move between the rows to find one another.

Long patches of dark earth, moist under our hands, clinging to our fingers when we sat and talked, and talked, and talked.

It held all of our secrets, that stretch of land.

It hid our steps as we raced back and forth, desperate to share secrets, to laugh, to just *be*.

When we were boys, we'd hidden treasures there. Told stories. Snuck a drink or two. When we were men, it became a refuge from all the hard parts of life. A place to be together, where no one would question a thing.

Where we didn't question a thing.

I missed seeing the tall rows, seeing how they were just green nubs at first, then by September, they were over my head, blocking my view of Sam's barn. It had been like the rows kept our secrets too, hid our path back and forth, kept us from prying eyes.

Now it was dead and gone as Sam.

"Y'all ain't supposed to be up here! It's private property!"

The taller of the two, this one more sensibly dressed in long sleeves and heavy boots, waved a dark gray box up and down near the broken doors, making a face as it squealed and squeaked.

The first man started towards me, waving down whatever his friend was going to say without even looking back. "We have permission," he said, his eyes weird and wild as they moved over my face. "You, um, your house nearby?" he asked, looking past me, downhill towards where my family's homestead still stood, one hundred years strong.

"Miller Talbot," I said, shoving my hand out to shake.

He hesitated, then just gave me a small smile and a funny little wave, barely a wiggle of his fingers. "Oscar Fellowes. The Jenkins family gave us permission to come investigate the barn and old house."

I blinked, surprised at his voice. "You're English? Huh. You've come real far, mister. And you're askin' after Terry and his wife? Those Jenkins? Hope you're not friends with 'em." I couldn't help the face I made. "Those two would've sold Sam for a dollar if they could've gotten away with it."

Fellowes looked a little embarrassed, his pale face flushing as he looked back towards where his friend stood beside the hanging door of the barn. "Well, we did pay them a nominal fee for their trouble…"

"Their trouble?" I laughed, though I could tell how bitter it sounded without even needing to see the frown on Fellowes' face. "Sam wasn't dead a day before they cleared out his place and had a real estate agent out here snooping around. That what y'all are here for? They trying to sell the place again?"

The other man had been taking pictures and doing something with a weird little box, waving it around and frowning at it, never really looking at me but kind of just… in my direction. He didn't answer me but took a longer look in my direction, his face a little sad looking. It sent a weird little shiver through me, that expression that wasn't pity but something close. "Ah, no. The farm has been deemed unsalable," he said carefully. "There's been some… complaints, you could say, that it might have some… problems that would make fixing or building a home here difficult."

"That sounds like a load of hogwash, if you don't mind me sayin' so," I chuffed. "This farmland's damn fine. The house and barn though, it's not so nice anymore. Ever since Sam died, hasn't been a reason to keep it up. But the land? It's fine as frog's hair." Fellowes' smile was nice when it came, warm and friendly. His friend was staring hard at us though, pretty sure he was frowning. "Your buddy okay there?"

Fellowes looked back at him and made a *stay-there* gesture. "He's fine. He just hates this part of the job."

"Real estate inspection?"

"Ah, well, we're investigators. Inspectors, of a sort," he agreed with a shrug, "but we're more interested in the history of the farm than the trappings." He made a small gesture towards the van they'd pulled up in, where his friend was lingering and another man with the wildest hair I'd ever seen was leaning against the hood, fiddling with something in his hands. "Sometimes we're on telly for it. People like to see us talk about the stories we find."

I glanced at the sign on the door of the van. UnReality was written in green and black letters. "UnReality? That's not a word."

"That's the channel that airs our show." Fellowes looked a little shy about that, shrugging again, glancing back at his friends. "A lot of people seem to like it."

I snorted hard enough to hurt. "If I can't get it with rabbit ears, I don't watch it. Though my grandson showed me how to watch one of those shows online. I can never figure out the little box he set up, so I don't get on the internet much."

Fellowes nodded. "Well. We're not here to sell your... friend? Your friend's place."

"Then why're you poking around his barn?"

He hesitated again, smoothing his hands over that ridiculous brocade jacket he had on. "Tell me, Mr. Talbot, how long has your friend been gone?"

"Ten years this December." It hurt to say it, to admit it was true. "Knew him since we were both knee-high to grasshoppers."

"Will the farms pass down to your families?" He'd turned his attention back to the crumbling barn, the barren fields. "Is there anyone who'd inherit the place, or does it have to be sold off?"

My turn to shrug. "Sam's kids, they weren't really made for the farm life I suppose. Mine are out west, but they'd come back when the time comes, I suppose. My eldest, he's got a degree in agriculture." And damn was I ever proud of that. When I was a boy, a degree in farming was unheard of. Though he told me time and again that it wasn't a degree in farming. Still... close enough.

Fellowes gave me one of those tight-lipped sympathetic looks I hated. "Oh, now, don't give me that shit. I'm proud as hell they're out there making their way! This life, it's not for everyone. Hell, if I'd've gone to school, maybe I'd have left too." I looked back up the hill, to the old shell of Sam's house. *No*, I wouldn't have gone anywhere at all. *Not with Sam still here.* Not with just a few hundred yards between us.

Fellowes nodded, turning now to face his impatiently pacing friend back at the barn. "I understand," he said softly, not turning back to look at me, something heavy in his voice that made me think maybe he was sad or near enough to it that it might make his eyes hurt with wanting to cry. I know that's how my voice got when I thought of Sam, when I remembered Martina on our wedding day, when I thought of… Well. When I thought of everything that I used to have, a long time ago.

"Yeah?"

"I think I do," he agreed. One of the men at the van called out, asking if he needed the box, and Fellowes waved him off. "I should go check in with Ezra and Julian." He sighed. "They get fidgety if I take too long. If you ask me," he added with a sharp, funny grin, "I think they just worry I'm talking about them." He waved, turning to head towards the van.

"Hey!" I called after him. He stopped and turned, giving me a small smile again. "What kind of history y'all lookin' for? Maybe I can help."

Oscar nodded. "I think you could. Might we stop in tomorrow? Have a chat?"

"Sure, sure. I still keep farmer's hours so any time after the sun's up is good for me," I chuckled. I wondered if they wanted to hear about Sam too.

Maybe I could finally let someone know about him. *About us.* He'd been gone so long it'd be good for someone else to remember him too.

They mucked around inside a while longer, leaving me to stare at the hulking shadows of the Jenkins' place as the sun slowly dropped past the trees.

Finally, they left in the dusty van with UnReality Channel painted on the side, a third man loping around the back from the driver's seat, waving his hands like he couldn't talk without the potential to smack someone across the jaw.

I was so lost in my own head that I didn't remember the walk back to my place across the sloping lawn, past Martina's old flower beds and small vegetable garden. Most of the Talbot farmstead spread down towards the river, in front of the house, leaving the back garden free for my wife—well, back when she was living anyway—to grow whatever she liked so long as it wasn't soybeans, she'd said. The rusted frame of Jack and Nedra's swing-set waited by the shed for me to tear it down, set up the new, safe one for the grandkids. *Tomorrow*, I reminded myself. *Have to do it tomorrow so the kids can play when they come visit next week.*

The house was dark, and I didn't bother to turn on the light, stopping in the kitchen to look back towards Sam's place. A flicker of light caught in the barn, and, for just a minute, my heart leaped in my chest. It was so familiar, his signal to me when his folks were finally asleep and we could run out together, getting into mischief when we were small. Then, years later, hunkering in the barn together and… Well. Martina never knew, and that was okay. We stopped before I married her, before Sam married Sarah. After our wives passed, we both felt too old for that sort of thing anymore, but it didn't stop us from wanting to be close.

And we were. Up till Sam died in his sleep from a heart attack. All by himself.

I didn't regret much in my life, but I regretted he died alone. Though, in all likelihood, that was going to be the way I went, too.

"No, it's not."

I stopped in the hallway between the kitchen and the living room.

"You won't be alone."

I flipped the switch for the overheads, the bright white bulbs

Jack put in for me last time he was home flooding the small space with light.

No one was there.

"Great. Not only am I old, but I'm also going crazy and hearing Sam's voice. Perfect." I left the lights on as I got settled for the night, looking back towards the barn one more time.

No lights flickered this time.

The laughing started around dawn. Familiar laughter. Kids cackling it up about something I couldn't make out, but it was too early for them to be playing like that.

I grabbed my boots, shoving them on as I fumbled towards the door. No kids lived out as far as my place, so anyone out there was up to no good. The morning was cool and damp in the way it could be down near the river, threads of mist weaving around my legs as I followed the laughing towards the road. I didn't see a single car in either direction as I reached the wide dirt track of Corley Road, but the rustle of the roadside shrubs and the loud peals of laughter drew me down to the left, towards the river.

"Y'all need to keep away from the water," I called out. "It's deep down at the bend there!"

We'd lost Freddie Montgomery when I was twelve, caught in the currents at the bend, and I'd never forget his mama's screams when the men pulled him out.

"Where y'all at?" I demanded, pushing into the overgrown bushes and weeds that hid the old track down to the dock that had collapsed years ago, before I even married Martina. "You kids need to show yourselves!"

The laughing stopped, and the world glittered. Not just mica specks but sharp, rainbow prisms of light knifing through the shadows. The path was wide, smooth, and clear. Ahead of me, a group of kids were moving, running back and forth, laughing silently like a TV with the sound turned off. One of them peeled away and darted for the dock, and that made me stop still. The dock was whole, and jutting out into the river, which was running blue and clear, not the usual chocolate milk brown it had been my entire life. The boy turned back and grinned, his too-big smile on his pointed face punching the air from my lungs. "Sam."

"Hey, Miller," he called. "Took you too damn long!" He started walking towards me and changed, passing through every version of him I'd known until he was the Sam he'd been when he died. He stopped in front of me and smiled again; this time the expression was just the right size for his face. "Hey."

"Goddamn, this dream." I laughed, shaking with relief. "This feels so real."

"It is," another voice said quietly. "Real, I mean. It's not a dream."

Fellowes stood behind Sam, his eyes closed and face a tight mask of concentration.

"What the Hell is happening?" I demanded, though I think I knew already. The air smelled of my grandmother's baking and sweet, fresh hay cut decades ago on a warm morning while we laughed in the sun.

"I got tired of waiting." Sam sighed. "You've been lingering, Milly. It's been time for a while but…"

"You've passed on," Fellowes said, his voice wavering with strain. "It's been a while, Mr. Talbot. You've been stuck here, and some people thought you might need help to move along." His eyes opened and were wild again, dark and sharp. "Your friend Sam came to us yesterday—"

"Sam," I snorted. "That's impossible."

"You know I'm always up for something impossible," Sam chided. "Remember when we decided to ride McSteen's red bull?"

"Christ, you broke your collarbone," I recalled. "I thought our dads were gonna kill us!" I couldn't help laughing then, and Sam joined in. A chorus of soft, silvery laughs drifted from the water and the trees. Fellowes' own thin smile dipped and bent. He was sweating in the cool morning air, his face pale. "You okay?"

He nodded. "It just takes some effort to keep the gate open sometimes."

Sam grunted softly. "Milly, Jack called these folks, this guy and his buddies, to come check out the place. Said he'd heard footsteps an' shit when he came out to clean the place up. Well. Looks like you wasn't ready to go yet."

I shook my head, hard enough to hurt. "No, you're…"

"Close your eyes," Sam whispered, pressing close like we used to in the barn that summer before Sarah and Martina. That summer before we had to stop. "Close your eyes and breathe."

I nodded and did as he asked. I breathed in—laundry soap and water, and sugar-sweet apples overripe on branches. Mother's perfume—every mother, everywhere. Laughing, bread, acid-sharp tobacco we'd pinched once and decided it made us too sick to try again, but we'd lie about liking…

"What happened, Sam?"

"That part I'm not sure," he said. "Time moves weird now. I was waiting for you, though. And I know everyone is there, just on the other side, waiting for both of us. Even Freddie. He's just like you remember, Milly. Just like. Hell, I'd bet you money right now, your grandpa's already got a domino game going and my Aunt Claire has a pan of cornbread for both of us. Remember how we'd eat it with buttermilk?"

I opened my eyes. Sam was a young man, and I was, too. The trees were in springtime, green and pale silver with tiny white buds that looked like snow. It had been summer when I got up that morning, dry and hot, dark green leaves ready to die and make way for fall. I looked up, and the very peak of the Jenkins' barn showed over the branches, whole. "What's gonna happen now?"

"Come with me and find out."

I thought of Jack, of Nedra, the grandkids I only saw once or twice a year. "I don't know."

"I can't keep things open for too much longer," Fellowes muttered. "This isn't something I do often, and right now…"

"Right now," Sam interrupted, "he's got his foot in the door for me. I pushed it open, he's doing his best to hold it. So come on now, Miller Talbot. Don't be scared. If you can swing off the branch over the bend, you can do this."

"Swinging off the branch over the bend was less terrifying."

"Yeah, but this?" He took my hand and lord, how good that felt after so long. "This is gonna be good. Everyone's waiting. And don't worry about the kids. They're not gonna be along for a while." He looked at Fellowes. "Remember, you promised—"

"This isn't going on the show," he said. "Promise."

Sam nodded again, sharp and sure. "Come on then, Miller. Let's see about that cornbread." He squeezed my fingers, and everything was cool and sharp, sweet and soft. And we were there.

LET'S MAKE A DEAL

Granny called the cat a moggie. Shaggy, mud-colored fur save for his brilliant white chest, a darling little heart-shaped nose, whiskers in which he demonstrated tremendous pride. The cat was Violet's platonic ideal of felininity. He waited for her at the top of the lane every afternoon, trotting alongside to escort her home. He came to the wide oak branch outside her window in the evenings, sometimes meowing in a way Violet determined to be cheerful, other times just quietly watching, cleaning his large paws and curling up on the brick sill as Violet went about her evening tasks of homework, then getting ready for bed.

Mornings were come and go—sometimes he'd follow her from the garden gate all the way to the turning that led to Grove Road Primary. Mostly, if the weather was fine, he napped in the tree of a morning. If it was too cold or too wet, Violet could glimpse him slipping into the garden shed or peering out from behind the wood pile near the kitchen door.

Violet named him Stephen.

"Who's this Stephen, then?" her dad demanded at breakfast one morning, rain sheeting down. It had never rained so hard in Violet's memory (well, maybe it had, but she had been very little then and not a big girl of seven, and she suspected her memory of the terrible storm was colored by her relative smallness against the weather) and she was worried. Stephen hadn't been in the tree, and a sneaky peek out the kitchen door didn't reveal him behind the woodpile. Her dad had been in and out of the shed earlier that morning, and surely he'd have commented if Stephen had been in there.

"A boy at school?" her father continued, dragging Violet's attention away from the lead-gray sky bucketing down. "Should I be worried, then, young miss?"

"A boy?" She made a face at that very idea—her Maman was always teasing her about this boy or that one, tutting over her little tummy, admonishing her about keeping her figure. Even Violet knew that was a ridiculous thing to take a seven-year-old to task over. Besides, boys were exhausting. So were girls, for that matter. "Stephen is a cat," she said flatly, distractedly. "He's going to get all wet out there. I'm worried for him."

Her father muttered uncomplimentary words about animals, particularly felines, and flipped the page of the magazine he'd been poring over for nearly an hour, something boring without a word scramble or find-it picture puzzle, with a very doughy-looking man on the cover.

They always wore striped ties, Violet noted, glancing at the green-bordered cover. Maybe that was a rule for boring business-men, that they had to wear striped ties. A cravat would be much more exciting, she decided. Very dashing and not boring.

Her father caught the direction of her glance and smiled. "That man will be prime minister one day, mark my words!"

She sniffed. "How lovely for him." She resumed picking at her breakfast, one eye on the dining room window, searching for a glimpse of a little heart-shaped face and fluffy fur.

Stephen hadn't made an appearance at the top of the lane, nor in the tree or the shed or the woodpile, by the time Violet returned from school. It had been more than a day since she'd last seen him, and that made her stomach feel fluttery and wrong. The house was quiet when she let herself in, which was unusual. Maman typically had a guest of an afternoon, Cook would be preparing tea, and Father, if he wasn't at work, would be in his office with a pipe and something sloshy and brown in a squat glass.

Port, she thought it was called. Or maybe brandy? Port was a type of wine. Yes. It must be brandy. She set her satchel down by the front door, and ignored the tiny twinge of guilt knowing she'd only annoy Maman by doing so (*everything in its place, Violet. Books, shoes, children! Everything!*)

"Hello?" she called into the quiet house, padding towards the kitchen. No lights were on. The fire was cold. The house smelled like spent pipe tobacco and stewed tea mixed with orange wax and washing-up liquid.

Ick.

"Allo?" she tried in French. Sometimes Maman could be particular, refusing to speak English with Violet until she was certain Violet's French was still impeccable.

A flash of fur and the shuffle-pat sound of running paws drew Violet up short. "Stephen! Oh, no! Come here, you little man! Maman and Father will go spare if they find I've let you in!"

The sound of paws on marquetry flooring gave way to a sort of odd little mewl, like Stephen was trying to be quiet but still wanted her attention.

"Stephen," she hissed. "Stephen, here kitty, kitty! Oh, drat! Where are you?" She hurried after him, in the direction of the mewl, stopping when she reached her father's study door. It was open—an unusual occurrence to be sure—and the smell of pipe smoke freshened, growing heavy and warm. Stephen, the little troublemaker, stood in the doorway, peering up at her with an almost satisfied look on his face. The sound of papers moving and something falling drew her attention away from Stephen. "Father?" she called out softly. "I'm sorry the cat came in! I'll take care of him immediately! Stephen!"

Stephen was a few feet further into the room now, watching patiently. His great green eyes unblinking, his tail curled neatly around his feet. One ear twitched towards Father's desk, tiny little head tilting. *Look. Look here, Violet. Look at what is there for you.*

"Father?" Violet whispered. He was still, quiet, hands folded on his stomach, chin on his chest. "Father?"

"Violet!" The sharp tone came from behind her, her father's bark of annoyance coloring the single word. "What is that animal doing in my study?"

Violet turned slowly, looking up at her father's annoyed face before slowly glancing back over her shoulder. Stephen curled around her ankles, purring thunderously. Her father was gone when she whipped her head around again.

"Oh…"

STEPHEN WAS GONE before Violet returned from the neighbor's, a nice older lady with some vague connection to nobility that Maman found impressive.

Stephen stayed gone for days, as far as Violet knew. But she wasn't really looking. By the time she thought to find him again, it had been weeks.

Maman hadn't come out of her room since the funeral. Grandmere had come from La Condamine to visit, ostensibly, but she showed no signs of leaving.

Father was dead, and the world, somehow, kept spinning.

People had to be notified. Papers had to be signed.

Mother had to be calmed.

And Grandmere had to come stay for a while.

It was noisy chaos for days. Then, suddenly, quiet.

The house was silent without Father moving about. Without Maman flitting through. The servants were dismissed—Grandmere had declared them unnecessary for the time being, given them all paid leave. She'd given Violet a ringing ear when she pointed out Grandmere had no place ordering about the staff.

Violet was alone.

Very, very alone.

And she missed her cat.

WINTER AND SPRING blurred into one long, colorless smear while the house was packed and they moved to one of the smaller properties deemed appropriate for a widow and her daughter.

Violet grieved Stephen almost more than her father. The day they drove away from the home she'd known her entire short life, she was inconsolable, struck speechless with panic and sorrow.

"Don't worry," Grandmere ordered. "You'll be able to speak with your papa soon. You need guidance. A firm hand. Your Maman will show you."

But, to Violet's relief and chagrin, Maman forgot about her.

Grandmere stepped in where Maman did not, guiding Violet in her abilities, steering her towards the correct path. Even when Violet didn't like it.

Two years to the day after Father died, Violet woke to a soft scratching on her window. Three floors up, no tree in sight, Stephen patiently waited on the sill for her to open the window and let him in.

"Stephen! How did you find me?" Violet knew it was impossible—they'd moved so far, and Stephen had never even been to London, as far as she knew. It wasn't as if he could look them up in the phone book. But it was *him,* and he curled up in her arms, and for the first time in a long while, Violet felt peaceful. Loved.

Two days later, her mother was dead.

And Stephen was nowhere to be found.

Grandmere moved to London full-time, the little pied-à-terre in La Condamine relegated to summer home status for Grandmere.

And Violet learned. Hours a day at Lauder Road School for Girls, where she was a day student, and evenings and weekends at Grandmere's side.

Nine years after Maman died, Violet turned sixteen and took to walking through London with her best friend, escaping the overwhelming presence of Grandmere and the lack of anything else.

Henry, her best friend in the entire world and the only person who *got it*—and also the source of absolutely fabulous gossip and many wonderful hats—had taken to making her go on walks to Mount Street Gardens where it was quiet and shady, and the dead minded their own business. Violet grumbled, but she did enjoy the outings. The house was so dark and stuffy, perfumed with too many vanilla candles and her grandmother's stewed tea. Henry had been her lifeline from her earliest days in London. He would never be so uncouth as to point it out, but Violet knew all the same.

"Seriously, Vi," Henry yawned, stretching out on the bench in the square. "Tell your grandmother you've got better things to do than go to Monaco this summer. Stay here with me! I've got clients lined up. You know you could use the pin money."

Violet huffed a small sigh. "I can't stay, Hens, and you know it. Grandmere wants me to meet her friends on the circuit this summer, introduce me to the right people and show me off."

"Again," Henry muttered.

"Again," Violet agreed.

"Your grandmere sounds like some sort of parapsychological pimp."

Violet tamped down a snicker. Instead, she elbowed him

reprovingly in the ribs and said, "Grandmere would go absolutely spare."

"But you want to stay," Henry noted. "You're old enough to stay on your own, Vi."

"Grandmere." She sighed helplessly. "She has a plan, you see." It was a very specific, detailed plan. It would have made Patton shudder in awe.

He opened one eye, giving her a gimlet sort of glare. "Are you afraid of her?"

"Oh, quiet," she grumped. Henry, who fancied himself quite continental, and this week was going by Heinrich whenever he introduced himself to anyone other than Violet, shook his head, letting his head tip back so he could catch a few weak rays of light. "You don't know how it is," she added, dejected. "Grandmere insists that I attend these silly meetings in order to—" she huffed, fading. "Oh, hell. You know how it is."

Henry lolled his head to the other side, louche and curious. "I know how she *tells* you it is, daring. But how is it *really*?"

Violet made a rude noise through her nose. "If Grandmere cuts me off, I have nothing, Hens. Nothing."

"I somehow doubt that. Your father's side is quite well off, and I doubt they'll let you suffer." He did, however, look concerned as he sat up, dropping his blowsy affectation. "Or are they still insisting you're, what was that phrase? Oh, right." He pitched his voice to affect a plummy Old Etonian sort of accent. "*Acting out.*"

"I spoke to Aunt Victoria at Christmas," Violet murmured. "She informed me that if I am to have any part in the family, if I expect them to extend any kindness, I am to find a way to deal with this illness, once and for all, as they refused to be embarrassed by me socially."

Henry raised one very groomed brow. "I'm sorry?"

"Aunt Victoria had a whole speech," Violet murmured. "I feel as if they were one step away from an intervention, but that would be a shade too plebeian for them."

Henry scoffed. "Your father had the sight, too! Stuffy old cunts," he muttered. "Hypocritical cows."

"But he was in finance, so that made it alright, didn't it? Because he never spoke of it or pursued it. Just ignored it when it happened." She sniffed, this time more wet than haughty. "So, you see, Hens, I have very little in the way of options."

Henry called Heinrich flopped back onto the settee, scowling. "It's ridiculous."

"But necessary."

He huffed. "If you say so. I'll just be dreadfully bored this summer without you."

Violet smiled thinly. "As will I, dear. As will I."

When Violet arrived at her grandmother's apartments in Monaco a month later, a familiar face awaited her.

"Stephen!"

The cat, curled at the foot of the stairs leading to Violet's little loft area, stretched his front paws, and yawned luxuriously, looking for all the world as if he had always been there.

"How did you get here?" Violet hissed, dropping to her knees and stealing a furtive look around the corridor to ensure no one saw or heard her. "Did you sneak into the packing crates? Oh my word, how—"

"Violet! *Attends! Maintenant!*"

She winced at her grandmother's strident command. "*Oui, Grandmere! Un moment, J'ai—*"

"*Non! Maintenant!*"

"Shit," Violet hissed under her breath, the heat in her face at the rare curse word uncomfortable and vexing. "Stephen, you can't be here," she cried softly. "Oh, I wish I knew you could understand me! Come, let me hide you in my rooms. She'll never visit there. It's too high up!"

Violet moved to scoop the kitty into her arms, but Stephen had other ideas. Quicker than his lazy posture would have implied, he was on his feet and darting down the corridor, in the direction from which Violet's grandmother called.

"Oh, blast! Stephen, please!"

When Violet arrived in her grandmother's private rooms, Stephen was nowhere to be seen, but her red face and gasping made Grandmere very annoyed, and Violet spent the afternoon practicing how to give elegant and refined readings to clients, practicing until the aloof tone and distant regard came easily to her voice and her precise movements with the instruments used for the séances were effortless.

In the morning, she arose to a quiet house and an unsettled feeling in her belly.

Annika, Grandmere's personal assistant, was in the front entry, snuffling softly into a pristine handkerchief. A man in a uniform stood beside her, looking grim but professional. "Oh, Mademoiselle Violet! I didn't want to wake you until... Oh!"

The man stepped forward, offering his hand. In French, he introduced himself and offered condolences.

Grandmere had died in the night, found by Annika just a few hours ago. She would be removed to the appropriate location and...

Stephen peeked out from behind one of the gauzy blue curtains covering the front windows overlooking the sea. His eyes met Violet's in a golden-green slant of something that made her stomach execute a slow, messy flip.

Violet was ill all over Grandmere's silk rug and Annika's leather pumps.

The next few weeks were frantic with arrangements, with Violet feigning confidence and grief (how could she grieve, she wondered, when she didn't truly know the woman who had been there for years, held so remote and aloof that Violet wondered sometimes if she had been a figment of her imagination after Maman died). Finally, she was returned to London. To an empty house that her father's family had nothing to do with, that had belonged wholesale to her mother.

And she hated it.

Hens was out of the country visiting some boy or other, and Violet was alone.

Except for the faint scratching at the front door that came every day at teatime.

"No," she whispered in the empty front hall. "No. I know what you are! You're a… a… portent! A harbinger!" She sank to sit on the bottom-most step, betrayal and grief warring for dominance in her heart. "How *could* you, Stephen?" she moaned. "I thought you were…" *my friend.*

It sounded ridiculous, didn't it, she wondered, to think of a fluffy stray cat as her friend? But he had been, she thought. The one thing in her life with zero expectations from her other than companionship and love.

And he hadn't been a cat at all, had he…

The scratching came every day, leaving no marks. And every day Violet sat on the step to listen, to rage at the cat and sob her heart out into her lap. What had she left, she wondered. No family to speak of, not even a damned cat, and she felt… lost. Empty.

Alone.

Even Henry wouldn't understand, she thought miserably. He'd think it was all a grand joke, or maybe just fascinating. His family had a banshee, after all, Violet reminded herself.

Nothing much scared Henry.

On the twentieth day of Stephen scratching at the front door, Violet dried her eyes, smoothed her skirts, and marched over to open the door. Stephen stared up at her, green-gold and unnatural eyes meeting her gaze. "If I let you in," she said flatly, "we must come to an agreement. Do *not* portend death in this house. Is that understood? I require a companion, and… and you are whatever you are, and I'm sure you would like a place to stay."

Mrrow.

"I missed you too," she muttered. "But what you've done is not nice, Stephen! If I'd known…" She trailed off. If she'd known, she'd still have loved him. A child's lonely heart reaching for a nearby friend? She'd have loved him dearly even if she'd known.

She was sure of it.

"But you must promise me," she hissed, "do *not* tell me of any deaths in the family! Do you promise?"

Stephen stared back at her.

"Oh, damn." She sighed. "Damn."

And Stephen disappeared into the house, quietly padding up the stairs to remain until Violet was much older.

Until a horrible day when he trotted out from behind the kitchen door, minutes before a police officer arrived to tell her of her son's death.

Not even enough time to brace herself, she thought distantly, the world suddenly too loud and too sharp and too close.

She didn't see him again until he was asleep on the foot of her bed one night. And she knew that she would find Michel already gone when she went downstairs.

"Please don't come back," she whispered in the dark of the study, beside her husband's cooling body. Stephen cocked his head to one side and padded under the piano.

"WHO IS SHE TALKING TO?" Oscar wondered softly.

Grandmere was not asleep, but she wasn't quite awake either. Some kind sister had turned the bells and beeps of the machines off to make the room less terrifying, the soft shuffle of feet in the corridor and the sting of antiseptic cleaner slicing through the faint waft of roses coming from the bouquet by the bed.

Her lips moved again, a soft whisper of a name, a smile.

Heinrich made a small, distressed sound and shook his head. "That damn cat…"

"What?" Oscar shot him a sideways glance. "What do you mean?"

Heinrich slipped his elbow through Oscar's and tugged him away from the bed. "Let's let her rest, my boy. She hasn't got long now, and I think she needs to tie up some loose ends."

Oscar glanced back as Heinrich led him from the room and, for a moment, was sure he saw a fluffy dark cat curled at the foot of the bed.

SOMETHING NEW

Grandmere was at her special meeting when I made it home from school.

It was Wednesday, and Wednesdays were for calling on her circle.

It was also the day when David and Joshua and their little band of ruffians decided to jump me and Ezzy in the choir room..

Sinjun had taken a look at me, rolled his eyes, and ushered me to the bathroom off the kitchen, in the servants' quarters. Which was really just his rooms, I suppose, after Danielle and Marcia retired and moved to Newcastle. Grandmere said they were roommates, but I had my suspicions.

I think they were kind of like me.

Sinjun frowned as he examined my eye and my palms. The silence made me feel guilty and kind of ick. I had to break it.

"Why do you still go by Sinjun? Grandmere said that's a base and common name."

"Madame is correct," Sinjun muttered, dabbing at the cut on my cheekbone with a bit of kitchen roll. "It's very base and common."

His lips twitched, though, and his eyes crinkled. "You're laughing at me," I said, trying my best to mimic Grandmere's imperious tones but sounding—even to my own twelve-year-old ears—sulky.

Grandmere always said sulking was for poor sports. I wasn't a poor sport. I was just angry and sore, and I hated everything about my school and Joshua Banks and David Davenport and… and all of my year. And the one above us. And below.

Except Ezra. Ezra was pretty awesome. And he got laid out worse than me but bounced back up and kept fighting.

He's my best friend. I don't know if he knows it yet or not.

Sinjun dabbed the split skin of my lip with something that stung like the dickens. "Laughing at you would also be base and common," he retorted, then, with a quick grin, stuck his tongue out at me. "Now, don't you try to hide your laugh, young man. There's nothing wrong with a good giggle now and then."

"Grandmere says gentlemen don't giggle, snicker, chuckle," I began, counting off the types of laughs on my fingers only to have Sinjun grab my hand and tuck my fingers down. "Hey!"

"You're twelve. A bit too young to be worrying about what gentlemen do and don't get up to, I'd think," he murmured, bending over the first aid box and producing a little packet. "Now this says it won't sting, but I suspect that's a fib."

I bit my lip as Sinjun cleaned the cut on my face. He hummed to himself while he dabbed at the blood, and I did my very best not to look in the mirror.

Blood was gross and the fact it was *my* blood made it extra ick.

And also kind of made me want to vom.

"Ez really walloped Banks," I said into the quiet. "Just sort of…" I lifted my right hand to demonstrate the way Ez had just leapt off the climbing frame and tackled Banks down to the ground. "Kind of like watching a spider monkey."

Sinjun snorted softly. "He sounds like a good friend."

I nodded slowly. "I think he is."

Sinjun hummed to himself some more, dabbing at my palms

and tutting over the bits of gravel stuck to my skin. "This will hurt."

I nodded. "I'm brave."

"Being brave doesn't mean you can't be hurt."

I sat as still as I could while Sinjun patched me up and eventually proclaimed me good as could be expected, suggesting an early tea and a sneaky slice of lemon pie for afters.

Of course I agreed. Be rude not to.

"What do you think you'll be telling Madame Fellowes then?" he asked, setting out glasses and plates on the tiny table in the staff kitchen. "The old *tripped and fell*?"

"I thought, perhaps… I would just go to bed early tonight."

"Hm."

He plated out some reheated Bolognese Grandmere would absolutely make that wrinkle-nosed face over, poured me some lemon squash, and himself a glass of water. For a bit, we talked of other things—Sinjun was a great football fan and had many things to say about United's efforts this past year. Finally, when the pie came out, he asked me, "And why did these boys think it wise to attack you and your friend?"

I shrugged. "They're wankers."

"Demonstrably. But even wankers think they have a reason. So, what was theirs?"

"They didn't attack Ez. Just me."

Sinjun waited, refusing to be diverted.

Damn it.

"They heard me talking to Sister Mary Elizabeth in the choir room."

"Ah."

I darted a glance up at him and, seeing his very narrowed eyes and his pursed lips, felt a rush of affection and safety. Grandmere loved me, but she was like one of those mother birds that shoved their babies out of the nest at the earliest possible convenience.

That's how Ezra described it, and he wasn't really wrong, I don't think.

"I'm assuming it wasn't so much anti-Catholic sentiment as they had an issue with you talking to a ghost?"

My face heated, remembering their whispers, the sudden, sharp bark of laughter from Banks as Davenport loped into the choir room and grabbed me by the back of my blazer. "I told them I was practicing my homework for Latin. Cicero," I added with a shrug. "Sister Mary Elizabeth tells me jokes in Church Latin and says it's good practice for me."

"And the boys didn't believe you."

Not even a little. I thought, when Banks had slammed me into the cupboards in the choir room, that I was going to die today. He'd been so casually violent. Sister Mary Elizabeth screamed but couldn't do anything. Not even follow me when I'd squiggled away, running for the lower school's play yard. That's where Ezra found me—found us—Banks and Davenport taking turns kicking at me and shoving me while their little gang of hooligans threw dirt and rocks, a few of the bravest darting over to take a swipe at me.

"I'm weird," I muttered miserably. "I can't help it."

"Do you think your grandparents are weird?" Sinjun asked, one woolly brow arching.

"Yes."

He snorted. "Alright. That one's on me then. How about this: are you ashamed of your ability, Oscar? Don't," he interrupted before I could get a word out, "repeat your grandmother's motto about pride in your abilities or whatnot. You, Oscar Fellowes, are you ashamed of your ability?"

I shook my head slowly. "I like it. It's… it's mine. Grandfather said Mum and Dad had it, too. And it's like… it's like being a Pokémon or something, isn't it?"

He didn't even bother trying to hide his laughter. "A what now? Oh, don't tell me—I can barely keep up with Downing Street much less whatever game you kids are into these days. Here, take this slice too. I don't want to have to chuck it tomorrow."

I dutifully took the last slice of pie—waste not and all—and was quiet while Sinjun rambled about some football club or other, meandering to the cost of groceries these days, bracing myself for what I knew was coming.

Sinjun wasn't good at being subtle.

"So, you're not ashamed then. Why did you lie to those boys?"

"Because," I said slowly, pushing the few remaining crumbs of the crust around on my plate, "they were going to hurt me."

"And they did, hm?"

I frowned up at him. "Obviously."

Sinjun pushed his plate to one side, leaning on his arms against the table. "You're weird, Oscar. And that's not a bad thing. Not everyone can talk to the dead, can they? That makes you remarkable. Why hide it?"

"Grandmere said people don't understand abilities like ours, and we should cultivate the right sort of circles and—"

"And." Sinjun sighed, shaking his head. "Your grandmother… Well. That's hers to tell, but your grandmother's coming from a place of, let's call it caution. Your grandfather as well but for different reasons. Now. What would happen if you didn't try to hide who you were? What then?"

"Then… people wouldn't like me much," I mumbled. "And I'd get made fun of."

Sinjun leaned back and fixed me with a *yes, and…* sort of expression.

"And Grandmere would be unhappy with me. And she'd make me do my lessons over and over again until I did them right."

Sinjun knew I didn't mean my school lessons. He knew very well that I had to practice almost every day with Grandmere—how to do a reading properly, how to interact with clients, how to present what she called my *best and most correct self* to the world so they would know that we Fellowes were forces to be reckoned with, that we were not some store front red hand fakers doing cold readings and fleecing the desperate.

"What did lying to those boys accomplish?" he asked patiently. "Did it make them see you as one of them? Forget they found you talking to thin air in the choir room?"

I shook my head, bruises throbbing in time with my pulse. "No. It made it worse."

"Then why lie?" he asked, gentle and quiet, reminding me of Grandfather for a moment so much it made my eyes burn.

"I just want to be normal. I don't like it when the other boys bother me about being a Fellowes." Drumming my heels against my chair, I blurted, "I'd think that in a city as big as London, Grandmere being a medium wouldn't be remarkable!"

Sinjun's snort of surprised laughter stung. "I'm not laughing at you, boyo," he promised, pressing one of the serviettes to his mouth—he most certainly *was* laughing! My scowl only made it worse, which made *me* worse. I slid down in my chair, wishing the floor would just open up and swallow me into the cellar where I'd live with the rats and bugs until I was old enough to leave home without it being remarkable. "Listen," he rasped after getting himself together, his lips twitching when he saw my frown.

Rude.

"Listen. You've been doing everything your grandmother instructs, yes?"

Slowly, I nodded.

"And how's that been working for you?"

"Fine. Great. Amazing."

He raised his woolly brows again, waiting.

"My abilities are... are good. I think? I mean. I can use them and they're stronger than her friend Heinrich, I think!" I sat forward, a tingle of excitement and pride helping soothe my hurt a little. "Sister Mary Elizabeth usually doesn't even talk to people! Not even Sister Bibiana, and Sister Bibiana has seen visions of saints before!"

I mean, surely, if Sister Bibs could talk to Joan of Arc, surely she'd be able to talk to the spirit of a dead Poor Clare in a school choir room, bored off her rocker and dying (ha ha oops) for conversation with someone other than a twelve-year-old boy?

"I believe those are two very different skill sets, Oscar. Though I'm C of E so I might be wrong there."

I nodded. "Makes sense."

"Your grandmother is… doing things in a way that work for her but might not work for you," he started again. "You don't enjoy hiding yourself away, do you?"

I shook my head, though he already knew my answer.

"Why don't you try something new then?" He leaned close and, in a near whisper and with a wink, suggested, "Don't!"

"Don't what?"

"Don't hide. They can't pick at you for being different if you're not ashamed of it."

I thought of EzraHe wasn't afraid of being different, but he still got bothered every day. And I said as much to Sinjun, desperation starting to tickle in around my nervousness. "If he can't be left alone, and he's all," I waved my arms, trying to convey just how awesome and badass Ezra Baxter was, "then why would they leave *me* alone?"

Sinjun sighed and sat back. "Perhaps I'm phrasing this poorly. They may very well still pick on you and bully you, but you won't be making yourself smaller for them. You won't be trying to shove yourself into a box marked *Socially Acceptable, Contents One Oscar Alexander Jameson Marsh Fellowes* for them."

"But—"

"Try it," he insisted. "Give it a day. And if that feels good, a week. A month. A year." He reached out and patted my hand, his rougher one warm and comforting and familiar. "And if it doesn't… Well. I'll help you get in the box."

"That doesn't make sense, Sinjun."

"Hush. I'm old and easily confused. Now, your grandmother

will be home soon. Are you going to tell her, or do you suddenly have a lot of things to do in your room?"

That was an easy answer. "See you later!" I said, shoving away from the table and scurrying for the stairs, Sinjun's chuckle following me to my room.

⌒

"Hey."

"Hey."

Ezra glanced up at me from beneath his overlong fringe, the dark bruise around his eye giving him a piratical air. "You look like shite," he announced, grinning. "Want to share my Aero?"

"I feel like shite," I agreed, dropping down to join him on the bench outside of the school library. "Ooooh, mint!"

"The best flavor," he agreed, breaking the bar in half and handing me part. "You get in trouble for," he motioned to my face.

"No. I hid from my grandmother, so she doesn't know."

He nodded. "My dad lost his shit." He chuckled darkly. "Said I should've won, but I'm a poof, so..." He cut another glance at me. "Is that why those wankers were beating on you then? You're like me?"

I shook my head and his face fell a bit, so I rushed to say, "I mean, I am. A, um. What you said."

"Poof. Queer. Bender. Gay." He snorted. "I'm twelve, so I'm not *doing* anything, but Da doesn't call me anything else now so..." He shrugged again. "Why were they beating you then?"

"Because," I sighed, nibbling the very edge of the Aero, "I talk to ghosts. They found me in the choir room talking to a ghost, and when I tried to say I wasn't, they jumped me."

"What?"

"Yeah," I muttered. "I know. It's weird. I—" I darted another glance his way. Ezra was staring at me with wide, excited eyes. His lips were parted like he was in shock but, like, happy about it. "I thought maybe… I'd stop hiding it?"

He nodded eagerly. "That. Is. Fucking. Awesome! And if anyone wants to give you shit about it, I'll kick their arse!" He shoved the rest of his part of the bar into his mouth. "You really talk to ghosts? Really?"

I nodded, taking a full bite of my part now. "Hey… Want to meet Sister Mary Elizabeth?"

"Who?"

"The ghost I was talking to in the choir room."

He was on his feet, dragging me by my hand before I could even get up. "Best. Day. Ever!"

Maybe Sinjun was right. Maybe trying something new wasn't a bad idea after all.

ROOMIE

"*Y*ou look stressed," Julian noted, handing me one of the takeout boxes. "What's up? Condo board already being jackasses?"

"I just moved in. Give 'em another week," I muttered. He snorted, pulling out his order and opening the box up. "I think they're giving me a grace period since the place has been empty for the past ten years."

"Jesus. I know you said it'd been empty for a while but a *decade*? Yikes, as the kids say."

"Do they though, Julian? Do they?"

He flipped me off, passing me my bottle of fancy pink lemonade with the real raspberry bits floating around in it.

"The whole thing was tied up with the estate of the woman who owned it before me. She died without a clear will so," I shrugged, "it took that long for her family to agree to sell it and split the proceeds."

Julian raised a brow. "A dead woman's condo, you say? Uh oh."

"Oh, hush."

He smirked, opening his bottle of elderflower lemonade. "Well, if that's not it, what's got you looking so frowny?"

"My gold earrings are missing."

Julian paused the dissection of his Waldorf salad, part of our delivery order from La Belle Jeunesse. "Which ones? You have at least a dozen pairs of gold earrings."

"The little rose-shaped ones I got for our thirteenth birthday from Aunt Minty. And good god, Julian, if you want to eat apples with mayonnaise, just eat apples with mayonnaise. Don't lie to yourself with walnuts and celery."

"Celery is an affront to god," he muttered, forking another piece of it aside. "And walnuts give me heartburn, but I like the flavor."

"You're so weird. Anyway. Earrings." I stabbed my own salad pointedly, making sure to crunch extra hard on the walnut. Because I'm a mature adult.

"Tiny rosebuds," he said, nodding. "She gave me matching cuff-links. And we got that creepy painting of us in old-fashioned clothes with those dead-eyed stares. Weirdest gift for thirteen-year-old twins."

"Aunt Minty is weird," I agreed. "Obsessed with twins."

We both shuddered. Even now, in our thirties, she gave us matching gifts and pouted when we didn't dress alike in pictures or at family functions. When I married Jacob, she nearly went into a tailspin about Julian not getting married at the same time, in a double ceremony. The fact that Jacob was an only child and had only straight, married cousins nearly gave her palpitations. Mother suggested sedating her just to shut her up.

I revisited that suggestion every time I had to talk to Minty. So far, Mother had refused to provide any of her personal Xanax for me to slip into the woman's cocktail.

"I thought we'd have to have her sedated when you got married," Julian said, our twin telepathy apparently still at work.

"Well, I'm supposed to meet up with her and Mother on

Thursday while Aunt Minty is in town to see that bone doctor of hers. They want to do a girls' lunch." I made a face

"Code for unseasoned chicken breast, plain salad with no tomatoes or carrots because they're high in sugar—"

"Dressing on the side!" I mimicked our mother.

"And then wandering the dying Galleria while side eying the poors."

"Got it in one. I'm arranging an emergency call from Harrison to get me out of the shopping, but I still need to meet them for lunch. And if I'm not wearing those damn earrings, I'll never hear the end of it."

"Maybe they're in one of the boxes you haven't unpacked."

I glanced around my new condo and sighed. There were absolute mountains of boxes waiting for me, despite having been in the place for nearly a month. The divorce had sped things along—we'd had to sell all of our properties and split the assets due to our prenup, Jacob's share going to pay his lawyers while he sat in prison. His lawyers then tried to make a play for my share to cover what his didn't.

Assholes.

"All the jewelry I didn't have to liquidate per the prenup went into my safe deposit box once we'd combed through receipts and credit card bills to prove what was mine because the jackass tried to claim Granny Gill's diamond ring, the emerald necklace Mother gave me when I got my MBA, and pretty much every bangle and pair of earrings I'd bought myself since puberty."

Julian sat back, folding his hands atop the table with his scowl firmly in place. "Look, I don't make this offer lightly but... want me to kick his ass for you?"

Only the tiny twitch at the corner of his right eye gave away that my brother was trying to make me laugh. "He's up for parole in like twelve years. If he gets it, feel free. I'll hold your watch for you."

Julian nodded gravely. "It's a deal."

"Give me your celery, and I'll give you my apples."

We traded plates, quiet for a few moments as we set to eating again. Eventually, Julian asked the question I'd been dreading. "How'd that date with what's-his-face go?"

Catastrophic. Demoralizing. Horrible. Bad. Ick. "Marvin. And… it went."

"Cec."

"He told me I didn't look my age, which I thought *oh hey that moisturizer is paying off! I need to send a thank you note to my aesthetician!* But what he meant was I looked too old to be seen in public with him, and he told me if I wasn't willing to get a laundry list of procedures done, I shouldn't expect any, and I quote *high-value man* to be willing to date me."

"Okay, so, new plan," Julian said lightly, pushing his plate away and leaning back in his chair. "I'm going to kick *his* ass first. Call Oscar and tell him I'll need bail money this evening. He knows where we keep it."

"Because Ezra?"

"Because Ezra," he agreed. "Seriously, though, what kind of monster says shit like that to someone?"

"Marvin Jergens," I muttered, stabbing at one of the mayo covered apples and imagining it was Marvin's beady little eye.

"Marvin Jerk-ins," Julian whispered loudly. We exchanged glances and apparently embraced our inner ten-year-old selves, dissolving into giggles at the ridiculous insult.

After a few minutes of coming up with increasingly creative nicknames for Marvin, we finally caught our breath and Julian said, "I know you're wanting to get back out there and whatever but—"

"I'm not." *Huh.* That felt good to admit out loud. "I'm not," I repeated. "I mean, it'd be nice not to spend evenings on my own when I'm between fundraisers and stuff, but… I'm really not wanting to get married again or anything. Not yet anyway. Maybe…" I poked at the apples, stomach unsettled as the truth of my wants and maybes floated so close to the surface. *He's your twin, for fuck's sake. He's not going to judge you! He's bestie number one, your favorite brother, ultimate ride or die even when he was being a douche like the entirety of 2009!* "I thought maybe I'd like to have a kid one day, but I don't need to be married for that."

Julian nodded, unsurprised. "I think you'd be a great mom one day."

"Not gonna comment about the whole not dating thing?"

He shrugged. "I mean, the track record's sucked so far—"

"Hey!"

He threw up his hands in defensive protest. "I'm just saying! But there's no timeline, you know? If you don't really feel like dating, don't. If you're not finding what you want out there, maybe just… wait a bit?"

"Wait and hope someone adds more chlorine to the dating pool," I muttered.

He snorted. "Exactly."

We meandered onto other topics until he had to leave to meet Oscar to check out a new apartment. They were making tentative plans to start splitting the year between England and the States, both of them circling the topic warily. First step apparently was getting a new apartment they actually liked and would want to come back to since Julian's current apartment was prone to maintenance issues that never got resolved.

I also suspected part of the criteria was *make sure there's room for Ezra to crash frequently* because, despite living with Harrison full-time, he sure did spend a lot of evenings sacked out on their sofa, he and Oscar like two overgrown puppies napping in front of shitty syndicated sitcoms whenever Harrison had to work late.

I cleaned up the remains of our delivery and, for the first time since moving into my new-to-me condo, was at a loose end. Julian coming over for lunch had been the only thing on my schedule for the entire weekend thanks to finally deciding to delegate more responsibility at work and declining a few social calendar activities.

Can't say as I was a fan of this whole *free time* gig.

Half-assedly, I unpacked a few more boxes, one eye out for those damned earrings just in case they somehow performed a feat of magic and repacked themselves without my knowledge.

Finally, when it was creeping towards dusk, and I judged it late enough to start getting ready for bed (seven p.m. is a perfectly normal bedtime, thank you very much, especially when I was planning on a night in with my two besties Ben and Jerry with a possible visit from my old buddy Captain Morgan). I showered, I exfoliated, depilated, serumed, moisturized, conditioned, blow-dried, plucked, and, for good measure, threw on a couple of under-eye, anti-dark circle, anti-dynamic lines (aka wrinkles) patches… and it was barely half past eight.

I was shiny and pink from the heat of the shower, my hair newly blonde after a few months of trying out bronde (which Mother insisted on calling *mouse brown)*. A few parts might be less… perky… than they'd been in my twenties, and some areas a bit softer despite the martinet of a personal trainer I saw four times a week and the barre and spin classes in between, but… I wasn't a total dumpster fire.

Peering closely at the mirror, I examined the faint lines by my eyes and the barely there ones by my mouth. My grandma would've called them *signs of a life well lived,* but I called them *my four p.m. Botox appointment next Monday.* But what if… I didn't? I squeezed my eyes tight, squinting through my lashes, and pulled a wide, grimacing smile, trying to imagine those lines growing deeper and more visible with each passing year.

Yikes. Not ready for that yet.

So, I smoothed out my expression, smeared on another lawyer of eye cream and some of that heavy duty hand cream before giving myself one more going-over in the mirror.

"Not bad for thirty-four," I said, voice echoing off the tiles.

I ignored my phone—a herculean feat made easier by the fact my charger was suddenly missing now and the thing was almost dead—and picked a movie from one of the cavalcade of streaming services I'd subscribed to, settling on my cushy Mario Bellini sofa to ignore my cup of tea and doze before I finally stumbled off to my room, unable to fool myself any longer about watching Liam Neeson saving his daughter. Again.

If I left the TV on for noise, so the place didn't feel so empty and I didn't feel so alone, no one would know but me.

IN THE MORNING, my earrings were beside my phone, sitting on my nightstand.

I DIDN'T WANT to admit it, but missing my personal cell was kind of nice. At least until lunch when I went and bought a new charger. My business phone never stopped ringing (well, buzzing, since what kind of monster actually uses ringtones anymore?) but not having a million messages from my mother? Or well meaning 'friends' snooping for dirt about my split with Jacob, or the whole trial situation?

Kinda nice.

Wednesday was the first day in a long time I didn't have a headache by noon, and I attributed that to the lack of my personal phone.

Ugh. Now I was sounding like Aunt Minty.

"Ms. Weems?" A knock on the door preceded the shiny, pale face popping around the edge of the door frame.

"I told you, call me CeCe," I said, smiling at the office's new intern. Tommy was the human version of a teacup chihuahua—tiny, with big eyes, perpetually nervous, and I suspected he'd bite at the slightest provocation. He refused to call me CeCe, but I kept trying. "Ms. Weems makes me feel like I'm your homeroom teacher or something."

He flashed me a tense, small smile. "Sorry. Just… your alarm company is on the phone. They couldn't get you on your personal cell. Your condo—"

I grabbed my desk phone and pulled up line one, waving Tommy off. "This is CeCe Weems."

"Sorry to interrupt your day, Ms. Weems, but this is Carol with Ace Plus Home Security. Your home's silent alarms have been triggered and we've notified the local law enforcement as well as your building management."

"Oh, shit. Could it be a bad connection?" I asked, already getting to my feet.

A pause, then, "I really can't say, ma'am, just that the alarms have been triggered and the necessary calls have been made. We recommend you do not try to enter your home at this time."

"Wait, alarms?" I jabbed the down button for the elevator, eyeballing the stairs. We were on the twelfth floor, but if the damned elevator took any longer, it was a possibility, even in my platform heels. "More than one? Not just like, the front door or something?"

"All of them have been triggered," she said.

"It has to be a short. My condo's on the top floor. The alarms are on the windows, a sliding balcony door and—"

"I can't say, ma'am," she repeated. "Please notify us after the authorities have made their assessment and we'll arrange for a team to come out and reset the system and, if needed, upgrade it."

She hung up before I could.

The entire drive back to my place, I did my best to convince myself it was a short. Some glitch in the line that made all of them trigger and not, say some weirdly coordinated group of cat burglars who were really into the collection of My Little Ponies I kept in my home office.

If anyone laid a finger on the Dr. Whooves or custom Canterlot-version DJ Pon-3 Julian gave me for our thirtieth birthday, there would be blood.

I was out of breath by the time I quick marched from my parking spot to the front entrance of the condo high-rise. Several officers were out front, one moving to intercept me as I approached.

"Miss Weems?" At my surprised expression, he smiled faintly. "Lucky guess. You look panicked and are making pretty good time in those shoes, so I figured you must've gotten the call about your alarms."

"Is it a short?"

"Ah." He exchanged a glance with one of his compatriots. "You'd better come on up with us. Just brace yourself, okay?"

Oh shit…

We rode up in silence in the tiny, 1970s elevator with its new-but-retro wood paneling and abundance of mirrors. "This place is very…"

I nodded. "*Newhart* meets *Mary Tyler Moore*."

"I was gonna say groovy, but that works too," he smirked. The door slid open on my floor, spilling us out onto the emerald green tile leading to my front door. Another officer stood outside the open door, fiddling with his phone as we approached. I could see, even before I reached the door, chaos had erupted in my condo.

"Oh my god…"

The officer who'd escorted me upstairs stuck close as I stepped into the entryway. Every electronic in the place was on, idle screens bright and waiting. My kitchen was… well, a *mess* would be putting it lightly. The blender was on its side, spilling something purple and sticky across the counter. Heat blasted from the open oven, warring with the cold pouring from the open freezer and fridge. Several bottles of alcohol were upended, caps off, and two glasses stood, neat and tidy, in the middle of my kitchen table.

The living room was only marginally better. Sheets from my

bed were strewn across the sofa, bottles of nail polish—thankfully unopened—scattered on the coffee table. A bottle of soda water had been sprayed all over the place from the look of things, and the balcony door was open, letting in the late summer heat and forcing the AC to work overtime. "I smell smoke," I realized, head whipping around to find the source. "Is something on fire?"

The cop nodded towards my bathroom. A dozen candles—most of them from a box of brightly colored birthday candles—stood along the edge of the tub, burned down to nubs. The tub itself was full of water to the very brim, the floor wet with overflow.

"Who did this?" I whispered to myself. "What the hell?"

"Ah, well," the cop said. "We do have some questions for you. Namely, do you know anyone who'd want to vandalize your home like this? Someone who'd leave this message?"

I followed the direction of his pointing finger. On the mirror, over my bathroom sink, written in Besame Forever Red lipstick, were two words: *Girl's Night?*

STAYING at Hotel ZaZa for the better part of the week had been nice. Or that's what I kept telling myself while I obsessively checked my personal phone (don't tell the productivity gurus) for messages from the condo's maintenance team. And it's what I told my mother and aunt when we met for lunch downtown. "It's a little staycation." I laughed. "A girl needs a break from the mundane sometimes!"

"A staycation doesn't usually involve work," Mother muttered.

"It does when you're me." I smiled, wishing I could manifest fangs for just a moment because I felt very bitey.

When I returned to my condo four days later, my old phone charger was sitting in the middle of my bed.

The water remediation people had taken care of the bathroom

overflow, and the cleaning service I usually employed had done a fantastic job in the kitchen and getting rid of the fingerprint dust the cops had left on everything.

The entire place smelled like bleach and that weird green toothpaste mint smell industrial cleaning supplies have.

I shut and locked the door behind me, feeling… not alone. Which was ridiculous. Because I was alone.

Very patently alone.

Not even a dust spider for company.

Julian was with Oscar and Ezra on location, Harrison was in Pittsburg for some meeting with a client, and…

And that was kind of it as far as people I hung out with outside of work went. And the fact the people were my twin brother and technically employees was, admittedly, sad.

So I forced myself to sally forth, to set my bag down, kick off my shoes, and pretend it was fine. And I wasn't alone in my fancy new condo on a Saturday morning and I'd still be alone Saturday night, Sunday, Monday… Well. And so on.

It was easy to pretend, once I sank myself into work and started returning messages I'd ignored while staying at Hotel Zaza.

By the time it was dark enough to go to bed and not feel ridiculous about it, I did.

So what if I left my lights on?

SUNDAY MORNING, my fridge door was open, and the flowers had been knocked over.

The word *oops* was written in a neat, even hand on my kitchen counter in margarine.

I swept the flowers into the trash and cleaned the smeared margarine up, then took myself to Bella's Bistro for breakfast before running errands all day.

Monday, I woke to my phone blaring The Go-Go's *We Got the*

Beat instead of my usual Peaceful Morning progressive bell alarm, and the smell of burnt coffee.

A puddle of too-strong dark roast marred my kitchen floor as the rest of it hissed and spit on the element for the coffee maker Julian had given me for our twenty-fifth birthday.

I worked late Monday night, crashing as soon as I got home, but not before I turned on the TV and every light in the house. Even my closet lights.

Tuesday, I woke to the chirp of my patio door alarm and the smell of White Shoulders perfume.

I called in sick, told Tommy I'd be working from home and to forward all my calls, then promptly grabbed my purse, my laptop, and both phones and hauled my butt over to Julian and Oscar's place, letting myself in with the For Emergencies Only key before shooting a text to Julian to let him know I was there and it was just for the day, while I sorted some things out.

My phone rang a minute later

"Aren't you supposed to be filming?"

Instead of Julian, Oscar's voice came down the line, startling me. "Sorry, I grabbed the phone from him before he could do the whole big brother thing."

"Technically, I'm older," I reminded him.

"Two minutes," Julian called out. "That barely counts!"

"*Any*way. I have a message for you. And you… might not like it."

I sat back on their overstuffed sofa, closing my eyes. Just what I needed—a production crisis. "Did Ezra get busted with a baggie? Oh god, did one of you punch someone?"

"What?" Oscar's startled laugh was high-pitched and breathless. "I mean, not yet. Which, put a pin in the bit about punching someone because we need to have a talk about this homeowner and how we need to handle people faking a haunting, but no, Lisa called me, and said she'd had a message from her brother, who'd had a message from their cousin Letty, who'd had a message from… Okay, you know what? Let's just say there's a grand game of telephone going on with the dead, and they're all trying to pass along a message to you, CeCe, from a Miss Rilla Coburn."

A weird, spinny, icky feeling settled in my stomach and made the back my neck feel cold and hot all at once. "I know that I produce a show about paranormal investigations. Several of them, in fact. And I am a believer. But what you just told me? I cannot wrap my brain around that."

Oscar chuckled gently. "To be fair, I've never had this happen to me before, either. The last time I played a game of telephone I was in nursery and everyone playing was alive." He paused and a piece of paper rustled on his end of the line. "I wrote this down to ensure its accuracy," he said, sounding a little amused. "Miss Rilla said she knows what it's like to be lonesome and on your own as a lady of means and wishes she hadn't scared you, but she was just trying to offer some companionship, one single, er, pardon the expression, ball-busting lady, to another."

Quiet buzzed in my ears, the silence itself a loud thing. My eyes were unfocused, the black square of their television shimmering and filling my vision to help me along the way to my new dissociative state. Only Oscar's small-voiced, "CeCe? Are you still there?" kept me from slipping entirely.

"What," I said quietly, "the fuck?"

Oscar, on a whoosh of relieved breath, said, "The old lady who used to own your condo is still there, apparently, and she wants to be friends."

"You've been here. Didn't you notice her around? Why didn't you say anything?" My voice was rising incrementally with each word, but Oscar didn't seem bothered. Instead of being defensive, he just chuckled, chagrined.

"Sometimes ghosts are, well, I suppose you could say latent. They're a background noise, metaphysically speaking."

"That sounds like Julian talking."

He snorted. "Rather. He's a bad influence on my vocabulary."

"He'll be thrilled to know."

Oscar's smile carried in his words when he continued. "Honestly, if I announced every background buzz of a spirit present but not active, it would be all I talked about some days. And Miss Rilla had apparently been quiet for a very long time. She felt drawn to you, however, and that made her more active."

To be honest, I'm not sure how I ended the call. What I said, if I said anything, was lost in a jumble of *what the hell* and *well, at least it's not a burglar terrible at their job*. I didn't realize I was heading back to my condo until I was in the parking garage, waiting for the elevator to the lobby.

Seriously, CeCe?

You're doing this?

MY CONDO WAS as I'd left it, but I had the distinct feeling of walking into a room and interrupting something.

The sound of fabric against fabric, barely audible over the AC unit, drew my attention towards the living room.

A pillow from my sofa was just coming to rest on the floor as I stepped into the room, flopping off the side and onto the rug.

"Miss Rilla?" I called quietly. "I, um. Okay this is weird. I mean, given what I do for a living, the fact I'm kind of freaking out here is weird. But... Okay, listen. We can share this space, alright? And I'll take care of it as best I can. But you gotta stop moving my stuff, okay? And..." I glanced at the kitchen, remembering the messes made there by my unseen intruder, and sighed. "Were you trying to make drinks for me?"

No response that I could hear.

"Look," I tried again. "Oscar passed on your message. And... And I'm sorry you're lonely. But I'm not. I—"

I...

I was a liar.

And somehow, lying to a ghost felt extra wrong. Like hadn't

they been through enough, being dead and all? Being ignored? And unseen?

Fuck.

Something fell in the bathroom. A soft metallic thump. Carefully, I padded over to peek around the open door.

On my mirror, in my favorite drugstore pink lipstick, was the word *Sorry.*

And as I watched, my tube of kohl drifted to the mirror and below it, in a steady hand, appeared the words, *Wanted to help. Lonely sucks.*

Fuck me.

Seriously. What the fuck…

"Miss Rilla?"

A cold burst of air pushed against me, then through me, shocking me to my very bones. In the kitchen, the blender rattled and the freezer door opened.

"No! Wait!" Startled out of my astonishment, I kicked off my heels and hurried to the kitchen. She had pulled out the packet of margarita mix, leaving the freezer door open as cabinets flung wide before my eyes. "Miss Rilla, it isn't even noon. It's too early for margaritas!"

The cabinets stilled.

"But… maybe… donuts and a movie?" I sighed. "I still have to work today."

The TV flipped on and my favorite streamer's logo filled the screen.

"Alright. You can pick something but nothing gory. No gore and no tequila before five p.m., alright?"

The menu was scrolling rapidly as my new (old?) housemate chose a film, and I hesitantly pulled up the delivery app on my phone. How many donuts did I order if one of us was metabolically challenged?

"Miss Rilla, after our movie we're gonna have a chat about boundaries, alright?"

The very faintest scent of perfume, something old-fashioned and expensive, wove through the room and a sound like laughing but too quiet for me to really hear followed.

She selected *Pride and Prejudice*—the good version, naturally—and while she didn't eat one of the donuts I'd had delivered I thought maybe she appreciated the effort. The entire time we watched (well, I'm assuming she watched), I nibbled a strawberry mochi glazed with sprinkles and she… she just was. And I felt her beside me, in the indent of the sofa and the waves of happiness that seemed to wash over me as the movie played out. I wondered if this is what Ezra felt, when he stopped trying to block people out. If the ghosts he encountered made him feel like he was bobbing on the water or maybe it was different for him. Miss Rilla liked me, for some reason. Maybe that was the only reason my walls weren't bleeding, and the cabinets weren't banging open and shut at all hours.

She was quiet while I worked from home, but after seven, I heard the tinkle of ice in a glass and the fridge opening and clos-ing. "Okay, okay, I'm done for now," I called out, padding from my office into the kitchen. She'd tried to make a drink happen but only got as far as the ice. "Thanks, Miss Rilla. I got it from here."

Perfume wafted past me again, and the light in the living room turned off.

"Goodnight, Miss Rilla. See you later. I have to work in the morning so maybe no door slamming?"

Somewhere in my condo, a door closed softly, and a quiet laugh followed.

THE ONE WHO WAITS BEHIND

"Legend has it," Reggie intoned, tipping his phone so the flashlight app shone under his chin and cast deep, unsettling shadows along the planes of his face, "when they found the bodies of Professor Leonard Quaid and Officer William Breaux, they'd shot one another in the *face*."

"Seriously? That's pretty dark, even for you."

"Julian, I heard you just yesterday joking about the death of Archduke Ferdinand."

"It was a satirical observation about how small moments can change the course of history and—"

"Whatever, dude. You're such a hypocrite. And I dragged your ass out here for a reason."

I glanced up at the hulking shadow of Clement House, a dark blot against the distant haze of city lights, and back at Reggie. "Oh? I must say, Reg, if this is your way of trying to seduce me, you're failing miserably."

Reggie's laugh was infectious, raucous, boisterous… Every -ous word you could think of, really. He didn't give me time to change my mind, standing outside the Dutch door of Clement House,

"

shoving me towards the dark entryway beyond. "Come on, Jules. There's no such thing as ghosts, right?"

"No, but tetanus is definitely real," I protested, pushing back. We both staggered sideways, Reggie's cackle splitting the night, startling the cicadas into silence for a moment before they kicked off again. "C'mon, Reggie," I whined, mimicking his own teasing tone. "This is ridiculous. Clement House is condemned, not haunted. Ghosts are—"

"*The product of overactive imaginations, unresolved grief, and communal storytelling designed to impart morals and cautionary information to the group at large*, yeah yeah," he shot back, repeating my usual talking points word for word. "But you're in Professor Norris' Folklore of Death class, and I know for a fact your entire grade this semester hinges on doing a research project based on local folklore. Clement House can't *be* more local *or* folkloric soooooo…"

I rolled my eyes, dodging his next attempt at a shove towards the broken porch and unsettling darkness of the old, condemned professor housing on the very edge of campus.

Clement House had once been a beautiful Georgian-style manse but was damaged badly by two successive hurricanes decades ago. The university had hemmed and hawed about restoring it due to its age, or just tearing it down. It had gone on so long that the county slapped a big orange sticker on the door and several on the windows around the perimeter of the downstairs level, but those were old too, eroded by time and weather and scraping fingers of nosy, bold students. Only the availability of easier to access sites had kept this from being party central, I decided. Who wanted to risk tetanus when you could just do keg stands in the basement of Jenner Hall? "I'm doing my project on grunches and—"

"And get in there, scaredy cat," Reg teased. "Before my buzz wears off."

And that's how I ended up standing inside the musty, humid,

stifling front entry of the old dean's house with Reggie making spooky noises outside and cackling thanks to being a fucking lightweight when it came to pot and bogarting my bowl of Strawberry Haze.

He never could handle sativa.

"This is Reg's idea of a joke," I announced to the empty house. Because that's all the place was. Not haunted. Not possessed, or whatever the rumor du jour was. It was a gross, dangerous, condemned house full of black mold and god knows what else. "I'm going to get a disease," I called out.

Reggie answered with a not very convincing *whooooooooooooo*.

"Fuck. Fine." Pulling out my digital camera, I fiddled with the settings to find night vision. "This is ridiculous," I spoke into the lens. "But Reggie has a point. Fine. Here we go."

I recorded the entry way, peering down a corridor that branched off just past the staircase. It led to a closed door that was warped with damp and age, a rucked-up carpet against the bottom. "And this is where I develop some parasitic lung infection."

A heavy thump sounded against the front door, followed by a burst of giggles.

"Fucking hell."

"Boo!"

"Reg, shut up!"

He giggled, still riding that high, and his heavy steps thudded down the old porch steps.

"Okay, so, this is Clement House," I began. "Everyone knows about this place. At least everyone at the school." I ran through the history of the place—the real history, not the folklore one—before begrudgingly adding, "And the local legend is that Professor Leonard Quaid and local police officer William Breaux were found dead on the second floor in an apparent murder-suicide shortly after Hurricane Candace wiped out most of this end of campus. No one had any suggestions as to why they were both shot, but rumors abounded."

A love affair gone bad—either between the two men or between one man and the other's wife—was the most popular story.

My own particular theory, one that I was sure to state for the camera, was that it was a load of crap. The house's demise was clearly on record as due to the double whammy of hurricanes, plus the fact it was already an old place when the storms hit one right after the other during the late seventies.

"While Officer Breaux and Professor Quaid did both die during the storm, there is no evidence that indicates their deaths were a murder-suicide. In fact, the only indication of their deaths at all is a brief notice in the campus paper and Professor Quaid's obituary in his home town of Lennox. Neither list a cause of death, and there was no recorded investigation into their passings, indicating that the deaths were not mysterious. I feel they likely occurred due to the storm, as several other people died during Candace either from the floods or damage to structures. The murder-suicide is a nice, scary story no doubt born from social imagination and the need to—"

WHAP.

Whapwhapwhap.

"The hell..." I lowered the phone and crept towards the swollen door. Was there an animal in there? Someone stuck? "Hello?" The sound like open palms striking the soggy wood sounded again.

And again.

And again.

And again.

Growing faster and faster the closer I moved. "Swear to god, if I get rabies," I muttered, reaching for the knob.

"Julian! Cops!"

WHAP!

The sound stopped as the blue and red flare of light broke through the gaps in the rotting drapes over the front windows, sparking in the dark entryway behind me. "Shit, shit, shit!"

I hurried, barely paying attention this time to where I stepped, slipping out through the front door to find Reggie crouched low by the porch steps. The flash of patrol car lights was blinding out there, throwing skeletal shadows from the trees and making it hard to see anything more than disjointed flashes of shape and light.

"They just showed up out of fucking nowhere," Reggie hissed, grabbing my hand as I reached the edge of the porch. "I didn't hear them pull up!"

"Come on," I said quietly, tugging on him along. "Run for it!"

The lack of sound behind us as we fled Clement House was a relief—we weren't being followed!—but the fact I couldn't see a single patrol car was flat-out weird. How had they gotten past Reggie, even stoned as he was? There had to have been some engine noise, something.

Reggie didn't argue when I climbed behind the wheel of his Jeep. We'd left it parked down the narrow residential street, just past a No Parking on Weekends and Evenings sign meant to keep students from jamming up the place during football games. "Fuck." Reggie giggled breathlessly. "Seriously, man, they just came out of freaking *nowhere!*"

"Remind me never to get high with you again," I grumbled, ignoring his giggling, giddy relief. "This was a dumb idea."

"Yeah," he agreed, sighing and going quiet for a second before laughing again. "But dude, you now have an awesome subject for your project. You're welcome."

"Jesus Christ."

We'd nearly made it to the end of the block when the flashing lights filled the car, blinding me and making Reggie gasp in dismay. "Holy shit, where did they come from?" he demanded. "They're freaking stealth or something!"

A heavy knot of dread squeezed the air from my lungs before sliding down into my belly. Reggie wasn't wrong—I was on scholarship and the rules for keeping it were pretty non-negotiable and included things like *Thou Shalt Not Trespass on University Property*.

Or something like that. I mean, it probably did. I couldn't see how getting busted for sneaking around a condemned house without permission and getting caught was conducive towards keeping my funding.

"Be quiet," I snapped, pulling over between houses and turning on my flashers. "Let me talk. You're high as giraffe balls."

"Oh my god, high as giraffe balls," he breathed. "I have to remember that!"

"Shhhh!"

The officer, when he arrived, was barely more than a weird disco shadow against the lights, the red and blue flashes making strange shapes of his face and the peak of his uniform cap. "Saw you boys at Clement House," he said, accent think with good ol' boy surety. "Y'all lost, son?"

I shot Reggie a glare. He was sitting up straight, staring at my window, eyes wide and glassy.

Fuck. He looked high as hell. I shook my head at the officer. "No, sir. We were just, ah, exploring."

"That place is condemned," he said, leaning a bit closer. The lights hurt my eyes, made it hard to keep them open, but I was able to make out a few features: sharp nose, soft cheekbones, a boyish sort of roundness to his face. He looked my age, maybe even younger, but his voice was rough, tired. It rasped over words, blurred at the edges like he wasn't used to using it. "I've had to chase kids out of that mess for my entire career at the sheriff's department," he added. "If it's not using the place for a drug den, it's trying to hold some," he waved one hand dismissively, "séance or other bullshit. Mind telling me what you two were up to, creeping around that place?"

"Not drugs!" Reggie blurted.

Christ. He was going to be a terrible lawyer.

The officer's hand dropped to his hip, fingers purple in the flashing lights as he tapped the gun hanging heavy there.

"I was filming some footage for a class project," I said, calm as I could. "I, uh, I'm a student at the university and Professor Norris teaches a class on folklore and death, and—"

"Norris," he muttered, a huff in the name like he was amused by it. "Cal Norris?"

"Um. Yes? Professor Calvin Norris? In the anthropology department."

He chuckled, but it sounded… sad, I think. Not like he found it funny at all. "I remember Cal. Real asshole sometimes. Good guy nine times out of ten, but he could really hurt if he wanted." He sighed. "He told y'all to come out here?"

"No," Reggie supplied, sounding a little less manic but still sitting stiff and still, scared spitless. "I suggested it. I thought it'd be funny to scare Julian," he pointed to me, "and also he needed to have a good project idea for Norris' class so—"

The officer dropped his hands, patting one against his thigh, looking back down the road towards Clement House. "The house is condemned," he repeated. "No one's allowed in there. It's my job to keep you kids out of there, keep it safe."

"Keep us safe," Reggie murmured.

The officer shifted, turning more fully towards the window. "Pardon?"

"Keep us safe, right? That's your job? Protect and serve?"

"Reggie, shut up," I groaned. "Officer, we're sorry. We won't go back, I swear. We're just heading back to the dorms and—"

The lights were too bright when he leaned in close, blinding me for a few seconds, leaving tracers and bright flares in my vision when he growled, "My job is to protect that place from little shit stains like you kids. Y'all are desecrating a sacred place. Come back again and I won't show you any mercy!"

The lights flared, then were gone. "What the fuck, what the fuck, what the fuck," Reggie chanted beside me as I scrambled to roll up the window in his old Jeep. Glancing in the rearview mirror, I could see the officer outlined in the glare of his lights, a solid white glow of his high beams and the strobe of the light bar that left him a menacing, stretched shadow with his hands on his hips, one near that gun, the other tapping against his belt.

Reggie hit the refrain. "Go, go, go!"

"Not a fucking problem."

I turned the engine back on—when had I turned it off?—and slipped into drive, pulling away from the glare of the headlights. The glow followed for a while until I turned out of the old neighborhood and onto the newer part of campus. Then it was just gone, the cop staying behind on his beat and letting us go.

We didn't speak until I pulled into the tiny student lot on Meechum, a few blocks from our dorm. A few clusters of students were hanging around a truck blasting rap music, and a few more hung out on the steps, laughing and shoving one another, pushing the call button trying to get a friend to come downstairs for some fun.

It felt good being around people again. Safer.

We were quiet for a long few minutes, neither of us ready to talk, I think.

Finally, I could make words happen without wanting to shout *what the fuck*.

"Reggie," I began.

He nodded, eyes fixed on the group at the dorm steps. Their friend had come out, and they were quieter now, clutched up together around one of them, gesturing and talking in hushed tones. "I'm sorry. I thought it'd be funny to scare you, but also I thought it would be a great project idea instead of the whole grunch thing because *everyone* does grunches and goatmen in Norris' class ever since he dressed up like a satyr for campus Pride Fest in 2000."

I closed my eyes, the flare of red and blue, the glow of headlights, dancing behind my lids and making my head throb. When I opened them, the world was darker and safer, no flaring lights, no hidden faces at the car window chewing us out.

No weird whapping noises against rotting wood, too steady and rhythmic to be anything but intentional.

I swallowed against my dry throat, nodding faintly. "Next time, tell me first, okay? And let me tell you about something called the *library* where I can research this shit without nearly getting arrested or worse." I opened one eye to peer at him.

Reggie nodded, quiet for a moment, then, "Julian, that whole thing was weird, wasn't it? I mean… the lights, the way he talked to us…"

"Cop on a power trip," I muttered. "And it's dark out, our eyes weren't adjusted to the flash of the lights, so it made everything weird."

"The thing is," Reggie said after a few moments, "his car was old."

I glanced at him. "What?"

"Cops don't use Crown Vics like that anymore. Not here, anyway. The cops down here use Chargers. They're smaller. Sleeker." He shrugged, fidgeting with his seatbelt. "That was a real old Crown Vic, Julian. Like older than us."

My heart felt weird, too fast and fluttery. I shook my head. "Brains are weird. You saw a cop, knew he had a car, so when you couldn't see it clearly due to the lights, your brain supplied you with an image of a police cruiser. Crown Vics are classic cop cars, so that's what you thought you saw."

"Julian…"

"Or it's possible it was just some dick pretending to be a cop," I rushed. "Thought it'd be funny to scare some college kids or something."

Reggie was quiet again, still worrying the seatbelt as if his life depended on it. Finally, he nodded once, jerkily. "Probably," he sighed. "Probably."

~

I STARED at the remains of Clement House, most of the top floor caved in now, the porch a heap of rotten wood and crushed beer cans, signs of small fires where kids tried to do something, spray paint marring the windows and parts of the remaining structure. The massive trees that dotted the front lawn still stood, though they were so heavy with Spanish moss that it was hard to tell where they ended and the moss began.

New builds encroached on either side of the old property, one new duplex built from the bones of the Victorian that once stood there and the other a four-plex doing a bad job of fitting in with the too-shiny paint and the black and white color palate popularized by those home design gurus on YouTube. Ezra made a disgruntled noise, fiddling with the camera as we stood beside the rental van, all of us staring up at the once grand manse that seemed to be forgotten by everyone but me, now that Reggie was dead.

"Surprise, surprise," Ezra announced. "Batteries are dead. The fresh out of the package, worked five minutes ago at the end of the block batteries." He shot me a glance. "You know what that means."

"Probable causes before anything paranormal," I said. "Bad batteries, a short in the connection, malfunctioning power indicator."

Beside me, Oscar whispered, "Ghosts."

I glanced around, a heavy and damp melancholy settling into my bones. "There's one I wouldn't mind seeing," I admitted quietly. I hadn't seen Reggie since shortly after our trip to Boo Con two years ago. I'd hoped… Well.

Oscar bumped his shoulder against my arm. "I know."

Ezra muttered a few curses at his rig before switching to a rechargeable battery pack and fiddling with the connection. "You can't stop me," he sing-songed to the space at large. "I have the power of god and technology on my side!"

"Which god?" Oscar asked idly. "Do I need to arrange a sacrifice on your behalf?"

"Not sure. I'll let you know as soon as they reveal themselves to me after a night of orgiastic excess and libidinous glory."

"Solid plan."

I shook my head, barely managing to hide a smile. When we'd gotten the request, via CeCe who received it from her PA, who'd received it via the form on the show's website, I wanted to refuse. Clement House had been a distant memory—buried under grad school, and that disastrous affair with Reynard, and a million other things—but seeing the name, the request from the university itself (okay, the assistant to the university president, but close enough) for an off the official record investigation, something not shown on the UnReality channel… Well. Here we were.

Beside me, Oscar was frowning deeply, staring up at the ruined second floor. "Tell me again," he ordered. "Everything about your visit here."

"My visit? That had nothing to do with ghosts." I laughed. Ezra snorted loudly. "Seriously. Reggie and I came out because he got high and thought it'd be funny. We got busted by the sheriff's department and the guy was super intense. We went back to the dorm, and that was it. No ticket for trespassing, no arrests, just a good ol' boy cop chasing us off after we were stupid and came out here in the first place."

"Hm." Oscar broke away and headed for the ruined front door. Exchanging glances, Ezra and I followed, picking our way through debris and creeping nature until we caught up with Oscar in the former entryway. "The men who died here, before the hurricane. It was violent. They're angry."

"That was a rumor," I interjected. "Trust me—I've researched this place. There was never any evidence they died by violence here."

"Yep," Ezra breathed, ignoring me. "Like they're breathing down my neck."

Oscar nodded slowly, gaze drifting towards the stairs. "Julian, do you mind if I…"

My face warmed even as I shook my head. Since my accident in Colorado over two years ago, Oscar had wavered between being exceedingly deferential to my new physical limitations and treating me like everything was normal.

Though I guess, this was normal now.

I couldn't go up the ruined stairs like I might have before, not with my bad hip and bum leg, not with the random dizzy spells I'd started getting over the past few months.

"I'll go with him," Ezra assured me. "You good, Hopalong?"

Ezra, however, had jumped right from a cautious wariness around me to taking the piss like nothing had changed. "Jackass."

"Love you too, babe. You complete me," he called over his shoulder, following Oscar up the rickety, incomplete stairs. "If we fall through the floor, make sure you get it on camera. You can monetize the shit out of that for our medical bills."

Alone in the foyer, I sighed, staring around the remains of the house. The university had been in the process of finally tearing it down after some frat boy from a wealthy family got badly hurt at Halloween but reports of "strange occurrences" had put a stop to the tear-down.

The form had listed things like bright lights out of nowhere, disembodied voices, shadow people seen out of the corner of the eye, knocking on closed doors from empty rooms, and the feeling of being followed or watched so intensely it drove away two tear-down crews.

All of the things could be dismissed with rational explanations. But here we were.

I shuffled my way through the debris with my cane, pushing bits of wood and trash out of my way. There was nowhere to sit and standing still hurt too much, so I decided to peek around, see what I could see downstairs.

The answer was nothing.

Nothing useful anyway. The door I'd been so close to opening before was now gone, the room beyond a mess of trash and graffiti, the floorboards half-torn up but piled neatly to one side. This must be where they started the tear-down inside, I thought. A few more steps brought me into the room. "Well," I murmured. "Past time this mess was taken down."

"I thought I told you not to come back."

"Shit!"

In the dark corner of the room, where the upstairs floor sagged down and created a soggy, moldy, cracking cubby of space between the rotten floor and the splitting ceiling, stood a startlingly familiar man. Hands perched on his hips, one on the holster and the other drumming away at his belt. I couldn't see his face, but I could make out the peak of his cap, the way he stood.

His voice.

Remembered anxiety and fear flooded my mouth with bitter copper spit. Suddenly I was that twenty-two-year-old college dork, sitting in the dark car next to my (dead) friend.

Upstairs, Oscar and Ezra had gone quiet.

Silence settled over me, muffling everything, as the man stepped closer, a flare of blue and red over his face. "What did I say last time I saw you, son?" he demanded quietly. "Tell me."

"You'd show us no mercy," I repeated, too many things tumbling in my thoughts all at once. *He looks the same. He looks exactly the same. Where the hell are the lights coming from? Where are Oscar and Ezra?* "We have permission to be here."

He huffed a laugh. "Not from me, you don't. And Norris is dead, so it ain't from him, either." He moved closer, somehow the shadows moving with him, the blue and red flare smearing his features. "Why can't you let us rest, Julian? Why are you here? Your little friends upstairs, upsetting him. You're makin' it real hard to do my job."

The movement was fluid and fast, one moment he was a shadow, a blur of light, indistinct features, and low, angry tones;

the next, he was inches from my face, blood and bone where skin should be down his left temple, gore I didn't want to name clumped in his dark hair. Gut punched by the sharp smell of blood, I staggered back, my hip and knee refusing to hold me upright. He followed me down, filling my vision, baring his bloody teeth as he leaned in even closer. "Let us rest!"

"Julian!"

Ezra and Oscar stumbled into the room, tripping over the detritus around us, shouting wordlessly as I thrashed. The pressure against my chest and throat was crushing, ice cold and growing ever heavier with each frantic thump of my heart. "All he wants is peace," Breaux howled.

"Let him go," Oscar barked.

Breaux jerked his head up, the mess of his face shifting into something almost lifelike. "Leave," he growled, the word broken, sobbed. "Just leave!"

Suddenly, I could breathe again. He was on his feet beside me, washed in the blue and red flashing lights that seemed to come with him. Somewhere, deep in the house, a voice called, "Billy? Billy leave them be. Come see me."

The lights faded. Breaux turned his face up towards the ceiling and smiled softly. He glowed, a faint white halo around him as he walked past me, walked *through* Oscar, then vanished. The smell of blood and death lingered on the air in a vulgar perfume for another breath, then it was gone too, replaced by rotten wood and mildew and something green and unpleasant. The room was quiet. Empty.

"Julian," Oscar breathed, picking his way across the debris-strewn floor, Ezra beside him.

Words clotted in my throat. "I… I, um…"

Ezra was already manhandling me to my feet, Oscar swooping in to grab hold of my other arm. "Get him outside," Oscar ordered grimly. "I need to have a word with Officer Breaux."

⌁

OSCAR WAS quiet until we returned to the hotel in town. Until after I'd showered and Ezra had downloaded the footage and EVP recordings and we'd all eaten. Then, he asked, "Do you want to know?"

I nodded. "Might as well."

"They were best friends. Close. He didn't say as much, but I think they wanted to be more. They died before it was more acceptable…"

I nodded again, bitter sadness twisting up with the remnants of fear in my gut.

"Professor Quaid had terminal cancer. He was dying. He told me he was scared and in pain, but Billy—that's Officer Breaux—promised he'd help. He asked Billy to do it. And Billy…"

"He wanted to keep his friend safe," I murmured. "I get that. He loved him." I thought of Reggie, dying of cancer too young—like there was ever any good age for that torture—leaving a gaping wound for me that only sometimes seemed healed, or at least scabbed over. "I get it," I repeated.

Oscar nodded. "Billy is angry—obviously—but when he's with Quaid, he's happy almost. He changes when he's with his person. But when he found you in the house, someone he had warned off before… Well, he felt threatened. No," Oscar corrected, "he felt as if you were threatening Professor Quaid. All Breaux wants to do, for the rest of their existence, is keep Professor Quaid happy. Safe."

Another nod. "And I appeared to be a threat to that."

He stared out the hotel window for a few more minutes before speaking again. "He doesn't want to leave the house. Quaid, I mean. He likes it there. To him, it looks just like it did when he was alive. And Billy isn't going anywhere without him."

"So, what do you want to tell the university?"

He glanced at me, a wry smile tugging the corner of his mouth up but sadness in his eyes. "Leave the place be. Let it rot into the ground. They're not going anywhere, but why rile up Billy when he just wants to be with his person?"

"Think they'll go for it?"

He shook his head. "Would you?"

I thought about it for a long minute. "If you'd asked me five years ago? No. But now?" He met my gaze with a sad sort of intensity, eyes red-rimmed and shining. "I get it now. And… yeah."

Oscar made a soft, thoughtful sound, and slid his fingers between mine. We stared out the hotel window for a long while, Ezra's murmured conversation with Harrison in the next room a comforting white noise under our thoughts.

"I'd stay behind for you," I blurted. "I'd wait. If I went first. I'd wait until you're ready to go."

Oscar squeezed my fingers. A quiet, answering *me too.*

A DARK AND STORMY NIGHT

"I thought you believed now," I teased. "What changed?"

Julian rolled his eyes at me. Even though I had my back to him, I know he did. I could practically hear those muscles straining with the force of his eye roll. "I believe in ghosts on an as-needed basis," he said. "If there's enough proof for me to consider a place haunted, I'll consider it haunted. I'm not just going to believe in all ghosts willy-nilly."

"What's this about ghost willies?" Ezra asked, bouncing down the rickety wooden stairs, just begging for a tetanus shot in his near future. "I didn't think you were going to tell him about the naturist ghost in the caravan park."

"The who in the what now?" Julian laughed. "Oscar, you've been holding out on me!"

I waved my torch at both of them, making them recoil at the flash of LEDs across their vision. "I'm going to fire both of you and bring on some of those greasy-haired blokes who shout at the spirits and accuse them all of being demons," I threatened.

"I knew you had a crush on that *Haunted Karaoke* guy," Ezra teased. "You've just been waiting for the perfect opening."

I jabbed a finger at Ezra. "Don't."

"What?" Ezra pressed his hand to his chest and affected an innocent, bewildered expression. "I was definitely not going to say anything about a perfect opening."

I waited.

He kept a straight face for just a moment more, his lips twisting into a smirk when he muttered, "Like the one you showed Jules last night at the hotel."

"Oh my god," Julian muttered, covering his face with his hands. "Oh my god…"

"There it is," I groaned over Ezra's cackle. "Both of you fired as soon as we sort this lot out. Did you set the equipment?"

"No, I was just upstairs admiring the view," Ezra groused. "There's two bedrooms and a study up there. And the corridor. I set the EVP device in the study since that was where the lights were reported, and the laser grid in the corridor, but I won't turn that on until we're set up there." He glanced up and shook his head. "I don't have your abilities, Oz, but I have to say there's something off about this place."

"It's an abandoned house in the middle of a swamp," Julian pointed out. "I doubt it's so much haunted as just creepy."

They continued bickering all the way upstairs, the three of us carefully picking our way over boards with dry rot and rucked-up carpet that was more mildew than fiber. The entire house stank of damp and rotten vegetation overlaid with a musky, bitter, animal smell I hoped was from some creature long gone.

"There are definitely spirits here," I said to end their argument once we'd fetched up in the study, a narrow room with bookshelves that had collapsed ages ago, scattering moisture-swollen books and papers that had been shredded by some small rodents to make nests or gods only knew what. Ezra set up the camera and a small light so Julian and I could do our spiel for the episode of *Bump in the Night* we'd come all the way out to Belmarais to film. Julian let me get through the basic introduction: the old Harbison house, located at the end of a very long and lonely road through part of the swamp the town was named for, had been considered haunted since shortly after it was built in 1910 when Mrs. Harbison died in a fall down the stairs. Since then, the place had been the scene of several tragic, allegedly accidental deaths, illnesses that took lives far too soon, and now mysterious glowing lights in long-empty windows and the howl and shrieks of tortured spirits.

Or, as Julian had it, swamp gas and mating animals.

To be honest, I was willing to give him that just based on the fact most spirits I'd met never shrieked and howled like some panto dame, and if they did, most people couldn't hear them. These sounds had been heard by over two dozen witnesses over the years, mostly reliable, including some out of towners come to hunt in the area who had no idea about the house's history or rumors, but I still didn't feel like it was the ghosts (three that I could count) making those horrible sounds.

"Right," Ezra shut off the camera for the moment. "Did we decide the master bedroom first or the—"

An ungodly howl split the night air. It rattled my nerves down to the roots of my teeth. Without realizing I'd moved, I found myself pressed against Julian, every hair on my body standing on end. Julian and Ezra weren't much better. We'd clumped together like scared rabbits as the howl hung in the air, some strange mix of animal and human pain clinging to the sound.

"Fuck," Julian breathed. "Maybe a screech owl," he muttered as the sound finally faded. "They can sound like screams. Or cougars."

Ezra shook his head. "That wasn't a cougar."

"Still could be an owl," Julian said, voice shaking. His hands on my arms were trembling, squeezing me so tight I knew that I'd have marks.

The howl came again, and again. "Shit. There're two of whatever that is," I realized.

"Okay, so maybe not an owl," Julian allowed, pulling me in as close as humanly possible. Ezra wasn't shy, either. I ended up sandwiched between my best friend and my boyfriend (okay, so, honestly, not so hot on that word, but calling him my lover sounded *so* late 70s European swinger and just no).

"Gotta be honest," Ezra said as the howls faded again. "Whenever I pictured this position, there were fewer clothes and less chance of imminent death."

NONE of us wanted to be the one to go outside and see what had made that sound, but none of us wanted to admit it. Julian ended up bucking up and announcing that, since he was our official skeptic, he'd go look around the area near the house and make sure no animal was injured or something. Ezra rigged a GoPro for him to wear. "Oh, good. Now when I die, you can post the entire gory experience on YouTube."

"Don't be a tit," I chided, though my hands were shaking as I helped him adjust the camera. "We're contracted to the UnReality channel. They get dibs on your death reel."

Julian leaned in to kiss me, biting my lower lip sharply as he pulled away. "If I die, mourn me for at least a decade before you even look at another man."

"I can't promise you anything more than a week."

"I'll take it."

Ezra and I stood back and watched as he let himself out into the absolutely sluicing rain, a flash of lightning making us all jump. The door swung closed on his tall, dark silhouette, and I felt a sharp pang of fear.

"What do the ghosties have to say?" Ezra asked quietly.

"They're here but not feeling chatty," I whispered. "They're old, worn thin. They've been here so long, I don't think they know they can move on."

"I should go check the EVP," he said. I nodded. Neither one of us moved.

"How long should we wait before panicking?"

"You? About another ten seconds. Me, I'd go for at least five more minutes."

The front door swung open as thunder cracked overhead, so loud it made the windows rattle. The man in the doorway was huge, easily six and a half feet tall, and broad enough to block out the ambient light from outside. I'm not saying I screamed, but if I did, it was definitely super butch and not at all a high-pitched shriek. But Ezra totally tried to climb me and escape Bigfoot there.

"You the guys filming the ghost hunt show?" Bigfoot asked. "Your friend out there said y'all had permits, but I don't recall seeing any come through my office."

BIGFOOT WAS SHERIFF ETHAN STONE. And we were apparently operating without legal permits. "See here? This is permission to film in Belmarais itself," he said, tapping one of the forms on the dilapidated dining room table. Julian, dripping wet and still wearing the GoPro like a sad, technologically advanced unicorn, glared at Ezra over Sheriff Bigfoot's bent head.

"And not to film specifically at this house," Julian finished.

"Afraid not. And as it's still technically private property..." The sheriff trailed off. "Look, I've seen your show, and I gotta admit I enjoy it. Y'all aren't like those others, and I appreciate that. Come by my office tomorrow morning, and I'll see what we can sort out for you with the owners. One of the Harbisons still lives in Sweet Briar, next town over, and owes my partner a favor. We'll get this sorted."

Ezra slipped upstairs to gather our equipment while Sheriff Stone and Julian made small talk, Julian tugging me closer to his side.

"I was guessing that shrieking sound was an owl or something,"

Julian said, shrugging. "I mean, we're in a swamp, so I'm sure there're all kinds of wildlife that makes sounds we're not used to."

Sheriff Stone went very still. He was still smiling, but it was one of those stiff, professional smiles I'd seen a hundred times when people are busted on something they don't want to talk about. Usually, it was the exact nature of a dispute with a dead relative, or how they ended up with that relative dead in the first place. This was nothing to do with a ghost, though. None of the spirits in the house gave us a flicker of notice, and Sheriff Stone had no one hanging on him, demanding vengeance or even a simple message from beyond. Whatever Stone was trying to avoid, it had nothing to do with the dead.

"Well, there's been some wolf sightings out here," he said carefully.

"Wolves don't live in Texas," Julian protested.

Stone shrugged, his smile only a shade easier. "Just saying what's been reported, Doctor Weems."

Ezra came back with our giant equipment bag and the Sheriff ushered us out to our rented SUV. He followed us in his official truck down to the end of the drive, then waited as we pulled out into the road. Harbison House was at the very end of a long, straight road so his headlights shone bright behind us for some distance.

"What's he waiting for?" Julian muttered. "Does he think we're going to turn back or something?"

I glanced back to see if he had moved. I could barely make out the dark silhouette of the Sheriff standing next to his truck, with the door open. As I strained to see, a large dog loped out of the shadows of the swamp and jumped up to rest its paws on the sheriff's shoulders. "Holy shit, that dog is huge," I said, my vision blurring for a moment. We were almost too far for me to see him at all now, but for just a moment, I thought maybe I was wrong and that was a human standing with the sheriff, not the dog I was sure I'd seen on all fours trotting out of the swamp.

"This place is so creepy," Ezra muttered. "I'll be glad when we're done."

I glanced back again, but the sheriff had turned his headlights off. Maybe I heard another howl in the dark, but I couldn't be sure. I just knew, whatever we'd heard, it wasn't a ghost. And it wasn't entirely human.

GHOST STORY

A MEDIUM AT LARGE NOVELLA

CHAPTER 1

"Thank you, Mr. Baxter! If anyone has further questions, he'll be in the Tech Roundtable at two. Green pass holders have automatic access, but all other pass holders need to stop by the sign-in booth to request a one-time access pass for the event!"

I smiled politely, giving a little wave at the round of applause from the audience. Natalie, the host for the Tech in Paranormal Investigations panel, met me halfway across the stage as the crowd started to filter out and the other panelists unclipped microphones and started to chat with one another. "Ezra," she whisper-shouted. "Hey!"

Her hug was far more intense than I'd been expecting, but not unwelcome. What can I say—I'm kind of a touch slut.

It's part of my charm.

"Hey! I didn't get a chance to see you earlier," I said, squeezing her back. "I don't have to be anywhere until the roundtable at two. Want to grab a drink at the bar?"

She glanced behind her at her partner unhooking the speakers and got the up-nod in return. "Sure. Beck has this handled, so let's grab a beer! I've got so many questions for you about the improvements to the spirit box you mentioned!"

"Looks like we're not the only ones day drinking," I murmured, nudging her with my elbow as we entered the bar. A large group had taken up one entire half of the space, all wearing lanyards proclaiming their involvement in the convention. They were loud, cheery, and more than one of them had their phones out, recording what was going on.

"Podcasters." She sighed, the word infused with venom. "Swear to god, they need to come up with some sort of licensing board to regulate who can make one."

I thought of Julian's tipsy ramble the other night about how we should totally start a podcast. *It'll be like... like...* Bump in the Night *Unfiltered*!

I really should not have let him have any of my stash. Harrison gets the good shit, and Julian is such a lightweight…

"I'm prone to agree." I smiled faintly, following Natalie into the bar. We ended up at a banquette with a handful of the aforementioned podcasters and one of the hosts of *Lost in Translation: Ghosts of Ellis Island*. The bar wasn't crowded, surprisingly, but had enough of a low hum going that it made the headache I'd been nursing all day throb just a bit harder. "What's everyone having? It's my shout."

"Oh, no, let me," Natalie protested, but I waved her off.

"You get the next one. What would everyone like? If you don't pick, you're getting fuzzy navels. And I'll pick your drink too." That got a round of laughter, just as I'd hoped, and I winked at the podcaster whose ears flared red at my comment. It only took a few minutes to get the order—mostly tap beer, but two intrepid souls coyly suggested I pick their drinks after all, and Natalie asked for a gin and tonic. "They'll bring it over in a sec," I announced as I sat down. "Apparently, telling them to just roll out a keg isn't a done thing here."

"It's not a done thing anywhere," Natalie groused good-naturedly. "Now talk to me about this spirit box."

Natalie was one of the few people I'd met in the industry who loved fiddling with tech as much as I did, and, frankly, who could keep up with me when I started rambling. The few people with us who had an actual interest leaned in, but the others who had just tagged along because I was recognizable and marginally famous (it's not my ego if it's true!).

We sank into conversation about the refinements I'd made to a commercially available brand of spirit box before a few of the hangers-on drifted off (without getting their round. Rude).

"I dunno," I admitted, taking another sip of my beer, frowning as a wave of nausea washed over me. Ignoring Natalie's sudden expression of concern, I pressed on. "I think I'm going to build my own from the ground up while we're on hiatus. We don't start filming again until September, so I have a few months. About ninety percent of the available ones are just filler parts so they can jack up the price."

"Maybe you should get a ginger ale," Natalie murmured. "You look kind of green around the gills."

"I'm alright," I protested. "Calvin Klein, me."

She snorted. "You're not Cockney, dude."

I rolled my eyes and, in my best (awful) American accent, informed her, "I'm fine. I promise."

"Hmm."

"Hey, I heard you talking about switching the standard mic for a Zeit 47? I had a transponder that used the '45 and it was shit with higher frequency feedback," the guy next to me said.

"Well, the Zeit 47 has an improved filtration process," I said, shifting away from Natalie's intense stare and focusing instead on the guy—Marcus? Martin? Morty? Podcast Man, I decided. "And something that might help with the '45 is unscrewing the back and slipping in a desiccant pack. We had a hell of a time with our box getting all FUBAR'd from humidity when we used one with the '45."

Marcus—Natalie did me a solid and used his name when she asked if he wanted a refill—and I fell into an easy back and forth until it was time to head over to the roundtable. Natalie stuck close to me all the way across the lobby. "You really do look peaked, Ezra," she murmured. "Are you sure you're up to this? If you need to go back to your room, I can make your excuses. No one's gonna be pissed if you can't do this."

I stopped and turned to her, exasperation and pain driving me to be snappier than I'd intended. *"I would. I'd be mad at me. I'm okay. I'm just tired, I swear. Between flying in from London yesterday morning, eating nothing but takeaway since I landed, and maybe overindulging just a tiny bit on my herbal refreshment, I'm a little green, but I'm fine. It'll pass."*

She sighed, shook her head, and offered me a small, concerned smile.

"I promise. I know my own body." It was the perfect moment for me to add a snarky comment or something rude, but instead, I passed the fuck out.

"I'M NOT DYING," I moaned at Oscar over the rather shit connection. "I just had a seizure and Natalie—remember her from that YouTube channel, *My Haunted Toaster?*"

"Your girl crush," he teased. "If I didn't know better, I'd think Harrison should've been a bit worried back in January of last year when you found that one. *Natalie's so fucking brill, Oscar! Oh my god, that's amazing! Come look at this build! Ozzy, Natalie West emailed me back! Oh my god!*"

"Fuck, and I cannot stress this enough, yourself," I muttered. Oscar cackled, and in the background, I could hear Julian's sleepy voice asking what was going on. "I appreciate someone who speaks tech, thank you very much, and Natalie and her partner are fluent."

"And," Oscar put in quickly, before I could derail him, "she's also one of my favorite people because she called me and ignored you when you tried to tell her you were fine."

"I don't remember any of that."

Oscar was quiet for a long, long time. Julian rustled around in the bed, his sleep murmurs, while not romantic, feeling too intimate for me to hear. A slice of a life I wasn't part of. And it made me miss Harrison even more than I had been. He slept like a stone, and I was the restless one, but I would've given my left nut for him to be in bed next to me right that second, snoring away while I fussed and tossed, a warm solid presence that felt like an anchor, keeping me from drifting away in my own head.

Harrison, when I let myself feel him, was pink and warm red, cool blue and green, a thin ribbon of yellow worry. Bold, deep ocean-colored confidence. The smallest fragments of pale uncertainty that pulsed and grew when I had one of my spells.

That yellow, those pale fragments. They'd widen and grow if they knew I'd had another seizure.

That it had been the worst one I'd had in a very long time.

And maybe today would be the day those pale fragments and yellow ribbon would twist and tangle with the reds and pinks, with those calm blues and greens, tangle and knot until they were one giant snarl. And today would be the day he decided I was too much to deal with. Too disruptive. Too dramatic. Too everything.

"I would prefer not to see you in a professional capacity," Oscar said after a long moment. "It would be very awkward for the both of us."

"Well." I tried for a teasing and jovial tone, but knew I missed by a mile. "I assume you'd wait until I got settled, then yell at me a bit for popping my clogs before you. Wasn't that always the deal?

You'd go first and make sure I got across okay when it was my turn?"

"Don't joke," he snapped. "Natalie said she couldn't rouse you, Ezra. They wanted to call 911, but someone noticed your bracelet."

I glanced at the burnished silver tag on the thick black strap Harrison had given me almost a year ago. It was a simple medical alert bracelet with that caduceus symbol on one side and the words *seizure disorder—see other side* below it. On the other side was another flat metal tag with a smaller engraving, three instructions in case I had a spell around people who didn't know. *Do not call 911 if seizure lasts less than five minutes, unless I stop breathing, or do not rouse. My name is Ezra.* "Remind me to tell Harrison thank you again for this."

"Tell him yourself when you call him later," he shot back. "Ezra, I know you don't want to go to the doctor for this, but—"

"But I've been to the doctors enough times in my life, Ozzy. You know that. One more grippy sock vacation and I'll need a new punch card."

"This isn't like your parents, Ez. No one is having you sectioned."

It was visceral and hot, old fear and panic erupting like pus from a wound I'd thought healed. "They will when they see I've got some fucked up brain shit going on and I can feel woo-woo weird vibes!"

Oscar sucked in a breath, letting it out slowly and softly. "Do you really think that? Ezzy…"

"What I think is that this mess in my head is mine to live with," I said, suddenly very tired. My hotel room was too cold, and Natalie had left me water and some snacks on the nightstand, but it was too far to reach. All I wanted to do was sleep, let this throbbing in my head settle, and wake up tomorrow to go home after the closing panels on DIY-ing your own investigative tools.

And yes, I knew how childish I sounded, whining even to myself and mentally stamping my foot. And Oscar knew it too, because when he spoke again, it was in that patient tone he got when people were being ridiculous and he felt bad for them. And it stung, to hear it used on me.

"They won't be able to see your abilities on a scan, Ezra. When I fell from the pier, remember? When we were fifteen?"

I nodded, even though he couldn't see me. "You broke your collarbone. I thought you were dead." It had been terrifying. One second, Oscar was beside me, the next he was on the rocks below the old pier. The ghost he'd been talking to never did come back, he said.

"Remember that I had to have those X-rays and MRIs and the CT scan?"

I smiled faintly, closing my eyes against the screaming pain in my head. *"Mr. Fellowes, your head is unremarkable."* I mimicked the dry, bored voice of the attending physician who'd seen him in A&E.

"Years later and Julian will claim otherwise," he said primly, startling a snort out of me. "If you're afraid of them finding out you're different…"

"It's not that." I sighed. Oscar waited. Finally, I murmured, "What if whatever's causing this is… it's something? And they can fix it, but it changes me?"

Oscar was quiet for a long moment. "Like you lose your abilities?"

"Maybe," I admitted sullenly. "Or I'm just different. It'd make my parents happy, wouldn't it?"

"Fuck your parents," he snapped. "And Ezzy, no matter what happens, I love you, you arse. And I'm not going anywhere."

"But what if I do?" What if I die? What if I find out and have to be a living ghost until my body catches up? My mouth was dry and my throat ached, words dying before I could get them out.

But Oscar knew. Or suspected. And he didn't have anything to say to that.

He let me change the subject and let me ramble about the

conference, the flight from London, the heat in Houston, and how his plants were doing in his absence. He drifted off around the monstera.

The next morning, Natalie found me on the bathroom floor when I didn't go down to the panel.

CHAPTER 2

"Shit like this is why it's a bad idea to leave me alone," I muttered into the empty, cold room. My thoughts had been whirling in an ever-tightening spiral since I woke up that morning. Hell, it wasn't even a spiral anymore. It had gotten tight enough to be just a fucking blot of panic, no edges in sight. Natalie hadn't been able to stay, but I don't think I would've let her, even if she hadn't had kids waiting at home in Beaumont. The hospital had admitted me for testing after a shadow showed on one of the emergency room scans. I tried to put up a fuss, finally giving in when a particularly no-nonsense nurse had offered to call someone for me, like the funeral home.

Nothing like the threat of dying to motivate me, I thought miserably. My head didn't hurt as badly as it had before, but the dull ache was still there, caused by the occasional sparkle of pain that lit up my nerves with fire.

I stared at myself in the reflection of the paper towel dispenser. "Oscar's right. You do look like shit."

Even in the metallic surface, I could see my dark circles, how stark my freckles looked, how tired I was. And it wasn't going to get better any time soon.

"Mr. Baxter," the cheerful voice of Alexis, the round-cheeked cherub of a nurse who'd shown me to the room that morning, came from the other side of the curtain. "Ready to take a ride?" she asked, pushing the drapery back, the rattle of the metal rings on the rail spine-curvingly loud.

"I'd rather walk," I admitted, sliding to my feet.

Alexis clicked her tongue, pulling a hospital-issue wheelchair around with a flourish. "C'mon, I'm not that bad of a driver! We can race the kid from the next bay. He's in for a broken leg. I bet we beat him to imaging."

WE DID, in fact, beat him to imaging.

I'm not too proud to admit I cheered a bit.

His mother didn't seem to find the humor in it, though.

Alexis gave us both stickers from her pocket stash, so I think that more than made up for any indignities either of us suffered. While Jeff Morris was taken to X-ray, I was wheeled to the right. "Here we go," Alexis caroled, patting my shoulder as she set the brakes on the chair. "Larry will be doing your CT, alright? Then we'll head on over to the MRI, just next door."

I nodded, mouth dry. The CT thingy looked like a fucking Stargate, and I found myself wishing Julian, of all people, was with me just so I could point it out. He always did like a good sci-fi reference.

The faintest tinges of worry, of boredom, of annoyance, and interest wove around me, rising from Larry and from the tech student with him. I could barely discern their feelings from my own. It was always easier with the dead. They positioned me on the hard tray, went over the instructions, then closed themselves up behind the thick partition to start the scan.

"Hold your breath."

I closed my eyes, arms stretched over my head, and tried not to think about how many people had lain where I was, how many had died. How many were like the Morris kid instead, just getting simple testing for something fixable?

How many were like me and didn't know?

The MRI wasn't much better. I'd asked for sedation but hadn't been allowed—I don't know if they thought I was seeking or if it was an actually good reason, just that I was popped into the machine to raw dog the entire experience.

I'm terrified of close spaces.

Even with my eyes squeezed tight and the soft foam earplugs firmly seated, I knew my face was just inches away from the machine above me. I knew my body was in a narrow tube, that a little twitch would bring me in contact with cold plastic so close to my skin.

Good thing I'll be dead dead in a coffin, yeah? Imagine how miserable that'd be until I rotted away.

The banging of the CT stopped and, after an eternity where I wondered if they'd forgotten me somehow, imagining that the radiologist had dropped dead behind their lead wall or was getting a blowie from their girlfriend who'd slipped in while I was being tortured, the platform was finally moved and I slid out of the tube.

"We'll get you up to your room so you can get settled. Tomorrow's the PET scan, and that's a big one!"

Hospital days are slow and long. You always think I wish I could just spend the day in bed, watching TV, scrolling on my phone, reading a book, but what you mean is I wish I didn't have to do the bullshit tasks I have to do and I could dissociate for a while.

I spent most of my day watching *Golden Girls* (Julian was totally Dorothy), fucking around online, and reading one of the mysteries that Harrison had been raving about, and it was the most boring, aggravating, irritating shit on earth. I wanted to move, to get up and do things, to just *be somewhere else*. The monotony was broken by a visit from the aide bringing my food, a specially restricted diet due to the PET scan. "No carbs, no exercise, no fun," he sing-songed, depositing my tray with a flourish. "Hope you're not vegan —your form said you weren't, but sometimes there's a mix up."

I stared down at the tray of plain chicken, naked lettuce, and a packet of oil and vinegar dressing with no sugar added and smiled thinly. "Just like Mum used to make."

"I heard British food was bland, but lord help me, I hope you're joking."

"Nah, it's not that bad," I said, forcing a chuckle. "My mum's was, yeah, but overall? Nah. I'd give my left nut for chips and peas right now, though."

"Well, you can hit the vending machine tomorrow for a bag of Lays," he offered. "After the PET scan."

"Not American chips." That time the chuckle was real. "British ones. You'd call them fries, but they're thicker. At least the good ones are. So good under some mushy peas. Drives Oscar spare, whenever we go to the chippie. I get double peas and chips. He says it looks like puke, but he also thinks fried Mars bars are real food, so there's no account for taste."

"Y'all are so weird," he muttered, pausing to collect the empty cup from beside my bed and help adjust the angle I was perched on. "Now remember to call for someone to help you if you need to pee, alright? You're on bedrest until after the PET tomorrow, according to your chart."

"Roger dodger."

"So weird," he muttered, leaving the room and pulling the door closed behind him.

"*So weird*," I mimicked, poking desultorily at the rubber chicken. It was barely past five, too early for me to eat dinner, but with my choices being the sumptuous feast of bland protein with the barest hint of vegetation on the side or watching the hospital's native cable channel with its fare ranging from *Hospital*

Hospitality! (all about the gift shop volunteers, told in five-minute snippets) to re-runs of family friendly movies and headache-inducing cartoons, I opted for the super-secret third option of *fucking around on my phone and pretending I wasn't in the hospital for tests.*

This option, while it may seem the obvious choice, was actually the most high-risk. If I went too long between rounds of bothering Oscar and consensually sexually harassing Harrison, they'd think something was wrong. But if I didn't sound *exactly fucking normal* and so much as fumbled the proverbial ball, they'd twig to something being amiss and I would be inundated with calls until I caved and admitted that I was scared.

I opted to harass Oscar first. He'd texted a few times, asking for updates on the con and if I'd managed to run into Lisa's brother, who was supposedly there as part of a panel on modernizing automatic techniques via technology.

ME

Miss me yet, darling?

OZZY

Always, dearest.

Though Julian puts out, so he's my favorite.

ME

Le gasp! How could you? I'm so
heartbroken I'll have to go sext my BF to
feel better.

OZZY

...

...

...

Oh, shit.
My phone rang a moment later.

"Le gasp?" he asked before I could even say hello. "Are you going to tell me what's going on?"

"Can't a guy try something new?" I closed my eyes, suddenly overwhelmed by the smell of the food, the antiseptic, the starchy stink of the laundry and the faintest taint of burned coffee drifting from the nurses' station. The urge to be sick, the desperate desire to just leave against medical advice and let the chips fall where they may, were pulsing thoughts just behind my eyes, bright like neon. *They've got so much blood and bits and pieces from me already. Surely that's enough to be going on.*

"Yes," Oscar allowed. "But I know you, Ez. ?"

Opening my eyes, I stared at the whiteboard on the wall across from the bed, with my nurse's name and all sorts of other fun info, including a bright red warning to ***MAINTAIN DIET PROTOCOLS IN ADVANCE OF PET***.

Jesus. These people were almost as bad as the keto cult about my food intake.

"Nothing, I promise."

The quiet that fell was cold, sharp. It made the queasy feeling in my gut spread out and seep into my entire body.

"Ezra," Oscar said quietly, voice barely above a whisper. " You can't lie to me—it's not allowed. Talk to me, arsehole."

The pleading note in his voice sliced me open where the queasiness had missed. "I'm just tired. And it's not Harrison. I swear on that old copy of Playgirl we hid in your gran's attic in London."

"I still think we need to get a better holy book to swear on," he muttered, sighing.

I smiled, missing Oscar painfully. Which was ridiculous, if I let myself think of it, because all I had to do was say where I was and he'd be here in two shakes. After he'd got done yelling at me.

"I've just had a lot on my mind," I said, which was both physically and metaphorically true. The potential tumor situation was in my brain, perking along next to some spots you really didn't want to be poked around in, surgically or otherwise.

"Is it—"

"It's *not* fifty questions," I cut him off. "I promise I'll tell you when I know which way I'm jumping," I added. Oscar's sharp intake of breath made me grit my teeth and squeeze my eyes closed, the incipient headache becoming actual. "I'm not leaving the show." I sighed. "Promise."

"It's not that. Not solely that," he amended. "I was worried… I mean. I'd get it, if you were. But…" His next words were a panicked rush that he tried to keep to a whisper—Julian must be nearby. "I thought you were thinking of moving back to England without me."

Shit. "Oscar. We made a pact, remember? One goes, we both go." To England, anyway. Where I might be going, I don't think he'd be able to pop in for a visit much as we'd like, despite his abilities.

"I know. And if that's what you're aiming at, I'll start getting my shit together. But—"

"I'm not moving back right now," I promised. "Harrison would kill me if you didn't."

"Harrison." He sighed. "Can't forget Harrison."

"Ozzy-kins, are you jealous?" I teased, grasping for familiar ground. Giving Oscar shit was something I'd done for yoinks and only rarely did he tell me it was too much, too far. This time was no exception.

"Yeah, of Harrison. If I were in his shoes, I wouldn't have to listen to you lie to me about being in the hospital."

"Goddamnit," I muttered, everying in side sinking to my toes. "Natalie?"

"Natalie."

"Just so you know, we'll be back in town within the next twenty-four hours," he said flatly. "And no, you don't get to whine about it. I'm coming back. I... I can't leave you sitting there without me."

The *just in case* was unspoken.

"Well, don't rush on my account. I've got a cam date with Harrison in an hour or two, and then I've got a lovely evening planned of mini documentaries featuring hospital volunteers and wondering if my brain's going to leak out of my ears before I leave this place."

"Ezra. Don't joke."

"Who's joking?" There was an uncomfortable, stiff pause, then I had to ask, "Harrison?"

"I didn't tell him. That's on you."

"Shit."

When he finally let me go, my eyes started burning and my breath caught in my chest.

Not symptoms of my potential little passenger, but bad enough on the telemetry to send a nurse sailing into the room, still rubbing sanitizer into her hands as she came to look at my monitors. "I'd ask if you're doing okay," she smiled wryly, "but we both know that's a bullshit question in this ward, huh?"

I huffed wordlessly.

"I usually don't ask ridiculous questions. But the thing is, kiddo, part of the prep for this test is no strenuous activity. Now usually that means things like running and all that malarky, but something I've twigged to over my entire time here is that working yourself up and getting your heart rate spiking with anxiety? That can screw things up for you too. I can't give you any of the fun drugs to calm you down, but I go on lunch break in about an hour if you want an ear. Or someone to watch a movie with." At my bemused expression, she held up her lanyard with its collection of colorful pins. "Becky. Nurse Becky," she added on a throaty, raspy giggle.

"I'm fine," I assured her. "Just—"

She shook her lanyard at me, one finger raised. "I'll be back in an hour. No buts." With a firm nod, she turned on her heel and strode from the room.

The door swung closed slowly behind her, just in time for my phone to buzz with Harrison's incoming call.

CHAPTER 3

*B*ecky chose a sanitized showing of *The Fast and the Furious.* "See, most people just stop on channel one and think it's blank or something. But you gotta wait a minute and the movie will kick in. It's some glitch in the system or something. It's been like that for years."

"Ah."

She slid me a sideways smirk and handed me the remote. "Or you can put it back on *Empty Nest.* I understand there's a multi-episode arc about the one with the red hair having a crush on the neighbor or something."

I blew a raspberry at her but took the remote anyway. "Seriously, aren't you supposed to be back on shift by now? It's been three hours."

"Two and a half," she noted primly, reaching to gather our trash together. I'd finally finished my meal, and she'd demolished her sandwich and soda, apologizing for having *food with actual flavor* while I had to eat *cardboard and sad thoughts* until the next day. "And I'm good. If they need me, they'll come get me."

"Cushy job, then? You make your own schedule and do what you please?"

"Not as cushy as yours," she shot back. "Oh, don't give me that look. I know who you are. Most of the nurses on this floor do, and definitely all of the techs. You're kind of famous, Ezra Baxter."

My face warmed and, damn it, the heart rate monitor blipped with an uptick in my pulse. Becky cackled, giving me a grandma-heavy slap on my arm. "I'm not famous," I muttered. "Oscar and Julian, they're famous. I'm… famous by association."

"What's the difference?" she asked, stretching her legs out on the tiny sofa beside the hospital bed.

"Oi, that's meant for family," I said. "Last I checked, we're not related."

She shrugged. "I'm your granny tonight, kiddo. Sometimes we all need one, huh? So what's the difference between *fame* and *fame by association*? Far as I can tell, it's all the same. People either know you or they don't."

"People know me, but only because of Oscar and Julian. Mostly Oscar," I amended—loyalty and a bit of truth mixed in. Oscar had been known in some circles before the show, before Julian. Not many, but some.

She sucked her teeth, watching Vin Diesel intently for a long moment. "Still, if being famous is important to you, it's the same thing in the end, really. People know who you are. People get excited to see you. All that jazz." Her bright eyes cut my way again. "That's what you want, right? To be known? So, what does it matter if you're famous for being you or because you work with someone a bit more famous?"

"Who said I wanted to be famous?"

"But you want to be known."

"Who doesn't?"

She shrugged. "You tell me."

My heart was beating faster—that damn machine was telling

on me. And the heat in my face wasn't awkward embarrassment now but annoyance. "I don't! Not by just randos. I mean… It's cool when people recognize us, but I don't need them prying into my private life, yeah? Okay, the fan art is kind of cool, and the fics are a hoot and a half. And kind of hot, to be honest, but Jesus don't tell Oscar about that. He thinks people stopped writing them, and I don't have the heart to tell him there's a vibrant shipping community on some of the more, er, robust sites about pretty much any permutation of me, him, and Jules you can think of."

Becky shifted to sit on one hip, her lilac scrubs straining over her ample curves as she settled her chin on her hand to stare at me. "Feel better now?"

"Huh?"

"That was a lot to just blurt out. Feel better? I get the feeling you're one of those people who doesn't do well being quiet."

Another huff from me.

Becky reached out and took the remote, shutting the telly off, leaving the room in a humming sort of not-quiet that came with hospitals. Outside the room were voices and machines, and hurrying feet squeaking over linoleum, someone laughing too loud and sudden. But inside the room, it was muffled and soft. Dark, save for the light coming in through the windows from the car park and the thin sliver from the bathroom. "My specialty is oncology, but I'm gonna whip out my armchair psych degree for a second here, young Ezra. You want the right people to know you. Really know you. Have I got it so far?"

I tipped my head side to side. Not yes, not no.

She smirked. "I raised eight kids, six my own and two of my sister's. I know when someone is trying to act cool, kiddo. And I gotta say, you're failing miserably."

"Aw, fuck off," I muttered, that damned blush coming back. I was going to blow the blood pressure monitor at this point.

She rasped a laugh again. "There's nothing wrong with wanting to be *known*, Ezra. And nothing wrong with wanting a bit of notoriety to go along with it. You're only human."

A low, sustained tone sounded, followed by two shorter ones. Overhead, an automated voice announced a Code Blue.

"Ah, that's me." She sighed, pushing to her feet. "Talk more later, kiddo."

I nodded, but she was already running, disappearing out the door and into the busy corridor with a dozen other running feet.

After a long few moments, I turned the movie back on.

Then off.

It was only half past eight.

I was tired. I was scared. But for the past few hours, I hadn't thought much about the thing in my skull, snuggling up to vital bits I'd rather not have squished.

ME

Hey, Ozzybear. What's shaking?

No reply. Not for a long few minutes.

OZZY

How's Harrison then?

ME

Fine. WYD?

OZZY

Waiting for the car to Heathrow. Julian's stressing, so I'm trying to distract him.

I sent several eggplant emojis, a water splash, some peaches, and a pride flag.

Oscar sent a middle finger and a heart.

My own heart did a fuzzy little wiggle at that. I might be lying my ass off about everything being okay, but he still loved me, and I could pretend all was right with the world.

~

"Sorry," someone—I opened my eye to see it was Mikey, the tech from earlier—whispered. "Just need to check your connections. The machines are being weird."

I nodded, half-awake. I'd managed to doze off after texting Oscar and sending a quick, flirty message to Harrison, even though I knew he wouldn't answer any time soon. He was on some super serious trip to meet with a client, and it was all kinds of high-level big money shit, so that meant Harrison was face down arse up in being Big Important Lawyer Man. "What time is it?"

"A little after ten," Mikey murmured, seemingly satisfied with what he saw on the machines and entering the info into his tablet. "Need anything? Trip to the bathroom? Some water?"

I shook my head, then changed my mind. "Definitely a piss. I can do it myself, though. Been doing it solo since I was three."

"Fancy. But you've also been lying down for a long while and that can make you dizzy. Let me help you shuffle on over there, but you get to hold it yourself. Insurance won't cover the handy."

I snorted, a spike of discomfort shooting through my skull at that. It made the vitals jump and jerk in unpleasant ways, at least that's what the expression on Mikey's face told me. "I'm fine. Just… you know. Piss."

He helped me to the bathroom door and stood outside while I did my business and washed my hands, then returned me to the bed. Handing me the remote, he nodded up at the screen. "Pro tip: After midnight, they'll play movies with curse words unbleeped."

"Scandalous," I deadpanned, and he smirked back. "I don't guess there's a smoker's lounge or something, eh?"

"Not since the seventies. Besides, don't you know that'll kill you?"

"I'm in a hospital. I like my odds."

He paused in the doorway and gave me a hard, assessing look. "Hey, I get it. I see guys like you literally all the time in here. And it sucks, you know? The whole am I or aren't I thing. But I promise you, trying to insulate yourself from everyone? Thinking you're being all brave and shit?" He shook his head. "It's not gonna help."

I sighed, sinking back against the upraised bed and closing my eyes. "You sound like Becky. Is that something they teach you all in nursing school?"

"Becky? Who's that? A girlfriend or something? Gotta say, I totally thought you were Family."

I opened one eye. "Becky. The nurse? Plum colored hair? Lots of flair on her lanyard thingy," I added, waving my hand around my chest. "She was on shift earlier."

Mikey shook his head slowly. "Dude. There hasn't been a nurse named Becky here in *years*. Not since..." He glanced around, stepping closer to lower his voice and whisper, "Not since Becky Martinez *died* on shift in 2010!"

My first thought was *of course she's a ghost*. My second was, *fuck my life, can't I have a day off?* I don't know what my face did, but it sure amused Mikey. "Dude, I'm fucking with you! Becky's in the break room."

"I say this with as little respect as possible but fuck you," I grumbled. Mikey cackled, and I was unable to keep from grinning a little bit. "Alright, alright, you got me."

Mikey was still laughing when he headed out onto the floor.

I, however, was back to being a grumpy sod when Becky came in less than fifteen minutes later, her own grin sly and too amused. "Oooooh, I'm a spooky ghost," she intoned, waving her hands in the air as she headed for the sofa. "I've been haunting my workplace for almost twenty years because I didn't finish charting before I keeled over!"

"Oh my god. I think I love you a little, Becky. And Mikey," I added, chuckling. "You'd think I'd know better by this point, but I'm not like Ozzy—I don't see 'em most of the time. Just get the..." I wiggled my fingers, making a wide-eyed expression. "Woo-woo vibes."

Becky stretched out on the sofa, grabbing the remote from me. "What's the woo-woo vibes? I don't recall ever seeing an episode of your little show with woo-woo vibes. Or is that like the after-dark version?"

"Oh my god."

She cackled, turning the telly on to the movie channel. "You're adorable when you blush. Remind me of my oldest." Her laughter died, her smile slowly fading until it was something wistful and distant, pale blue and the faintest tinge of pink. "Ricky. Ricky is about your age. Loves a good laugh. And always a smart ass. Oh, here we go. *The Pacifier.*"

"I recognize a subject change when I hear one," I murmured.

"It's rude to point one out."

And there it was. A very faint tingle, red-blue-brown, of anxiety. Not my own this time. Anxiety and a simmer of anger that tasted bitter on the back of my tongue. But something softer… Love but not like I knew it. I could name it, but only because it felt similar to the love I felt with Oscar. Nothing like the bright and slow-burning red-purple-white with Harrison. Or even the softer, less hot, feelings with Julian and even CeCe.

This was something deep and infinite, and I felt ridiculous for even thinking those words. Like some sort of empathic freaking greeting card or something. My quiet must've been too loud because Becky reached over to give my arm a shove and raise her brow in question. "Mind's wandering," I said, shrugging. "Nervous about tomorrow."

"So, tell me about the woo-woo vibes then. Get your mind off the test."

"So… Ugh. It sounds so weird when I say it out loud to anyone other than the guys. And CeCe. But. Okay. You know how Oscar's a medium?"

She hummed in agreement, gaze intent on my face as that damn blush crept ever higher.

"I'm an empath. But it seems to work better with the dead than the living. Sometimes I can pick up on the," I paused to wiggle my fingers at her, "from the living but I've spent my life trying to train myself not to. I don't like knowing what my friends are feeling. Or strangers on the street for that matter. It's… it's too much. But the dead…" I shook my head. "They're easier. They're kinder."

She shrugged. "Makes sense to me. Besides, I think the dead need more empathy than the living."

"Empathy and being an empath aren't the same, really."

"Close enough." She winked at my frustrated groan. "Why don't you call your friend? Don't give me that look. Trying to hang tough with things like this? It's not good for you, hon."

"Oscar's on his way," I said, feeling a little pang of pride at the flicker of surprise that crossed her features. "He's impossible to lie to. For me, anyway."

"And your boyfriend?"

"It feels weird, calling him a *boy*friend," I muttered. "He's older than me, for fuck's sake. Nearly forty."

"You're avoiding."

"Take the hint."

She just raised a brow, waiting.

I shrugged again, sniffing, pushing my hair behind my ears, basically doing everything possible to feign disinterest. "Eh. He's got shit to do."

I knew if I called him, if I admitted to him where I was and what was happening, he'd leave Philadelphia on the first flight he could get. He'd be here before I woke up in the morning if he could manage it.

But he'd pulled my—our, if you counted the things he'd done for the three of us—ass out of the fire so many times. Hell, I was shocked he still had clients, the number of times he'd dropped everything to come running when things went pear-shaped. If he ditched Richie Rich to come sit in the waiting room and drink shit coffee and I was fine, then I'd never stop feeling guilty. And he'd have every right to be annoyed with me.

"I'll call him after the test."

Becky was quiet for a long, long time. On screen Vin Diesel did his thing, and I wondered how he had a career.

Finally, Becky whispered, "You really do remind me of Ricky. So much."

CHAPTER 4

At half past one, the ward was an odd sort of quiet. The background noise of feet squeaking on the floors, the muffled beep of telemetry in other rooms, wafts of coffee and someone's late night barbecue dinner were nothing. Ghosts of daytime shifts, moving through the nighttime hours.

Shit, I got poetic when I was waiting to find out if I was going to die.

Becky snored softly on the sofa beside me, her lanyard in a puddle of rainbow and plastic on the nightstand by the bed. My phone flashed with an incoming text—the sixth in twenty minutes—from Harrison.

"Fuck, fuck, fuckity, fuck, fuck."

Our conversation earlier had gone well. Better than well. I felt awkward trying to *do* anything in a hospital when Mikey or whoever could pop in at any minute, so we just talked. He tried to get a bit started but backed off when I complained of a headache. And I thought he'd believed me when I said my camera was being weird so we couldn't video chat.

"Shit."

"You okay, kid?" Becky murmured, opening one eye. "Shit. I missed the end. What's on now?"

"Ah, I think it's *Knockaround Guys.*"

She grunted in satisfaction. "Solid entry in his filmography." She wiggled her way into a sitting position before giving me an assessing look. "You need to sleep, you know? The PET test isn't super invasive, but it's taxing. And there are a million little things that can cause funky results, including not getting enough rest and your brain getting all wackadoodle from anxiety."

"Is that the medical terminology for it, then? Wackadoodle?"

"Don't give me that smirk, young man," she scolded, though her own lips were curved into a small smile. "Ugh, this movie calls for popcorn, but *one of us* isn't allowed to eat till tomorrow." Becky sniffed. "Way to ruin the fun."

I couldn't help it—I cackled. "You're a right one, aren't you?"

She winked, getting to her feet to grab a cup of water from the sink. "You talk to him?" she asked, nodding at the phone still out beside me.."

"Yeah… We're good. It's fine," I fibbed. . My empathic woo-woo stuff didn't work over long distance, but I was sure I could *feel* the red-blue-black annoyance and frustration radiating off of Harrison from here.

And I low key hated myself for it.

Wait until you know for sure. Then you can tell him. He'll understand. Maybe.

"I don't want him to worry," I muttered. "Everyone always worries about me. I used to kind of like it, you know? But now I just feel like… like I'm a burden."

"I wonder," she said quietly, sitting on the edge of my bed, "how many of the ghosts you've met felt that way?"

Conversational whiplash ahoy… "Huh?"

"The ghosts. On your little show. Did they feel like burdens before they died?"

"I… huh? Maybe? Some, I'm sure. Ghosts were people too, after all," I snarked. "Just because they're dead doesn't mean they're absolved of the feelings they had in life."

"That's what they always like to tell you during grief counseling. Well. Maybe it was just the one I went to, you know? *Oh, the dead don't feel anger. They don't feel sorrow. They're beyond that.* At the time, I thought it meant they existed in some perfect state of happiness or something but looking back, I think they were trying to remind us that dead is dead is dead, and corpses have no feelings about anything in particular."

"Do you not believe in ghosts, then?"

She smiled a little. I think Julian would've called her expression *wry*. "I tell myself I do. It makes things easier, sometimes. But to be honest, I'm not entirely sure. What if the things I think are a ghost or a visit or *experience* are just too much caffeine and not enough sleep? Or just," she sighed, spreading her hands wide and letting something intangible slip through her fingers, "desperate desire for that cold chill to be something more than the AC kicking on?"

On screen, Vin Diesel was mugged for his paycheck, and something went *bang*. Becky stared hard at the screen, but I knew she wasn't seeing the adventures of low-level mobsters in rural Montana. "What was he like, your Ricky?"

"Like you," she said, her smile forced and gaze distant.

"Oh, come on now! That's a cop-out, Becks. *Like you*. Phhhhh-ht." I threw up my hands in a show of dismay. "Entertain me. Tell me about him, then! You're spending the night up here with me for some reason, so make yourself useful. Keep me distracted."

She looked, for just a moment, mutinous before the smile became truer, a little bigger, a little less wistful. "He was an asshole, too."

That earned a snort. "You're mispronouncing *charming*."

"Yep, just like my little asshole." She chuckled, watery and soft. "Ricky... Well. He was stubborn as a mule. And hated thinking anyone felt bad for him or that he was being a *burden*. He never understood that pity and compassion were two different things, not when it was applied to him. He was caring and generous as the day is long, but if *he* was the one needing someone else?" She sucked her teeth, shaking her head. "Well. He just wasn't having it." She shot me a very pointed glance. "Sound familiar yet?"

I sniffed, fussing with the edge of the hospital-issue blanket. "Not at all."

"Hmm. Let's try this then. He loved fiercely. You know the phrase *ride or die?*"

I nodded.

"That was him. If you were one of his people, he was ride or die for you. All the way. Ricky…" She paused again, this time turning her face away fully, staring at the closed blinds rather than letting me see her cry. "Rick had so much love in him. So goddamned much. And he just poured it out on everyone he kept in his little circle. Me, his dad, his siblings, his friends. And protective? Whoooooo lord, that boy was like a freakin' honey badger when it came to people he loved."

The quiet that trailed her words was soft, heavy. Almost stifling. I was loath to break it, but finally, I asked, "So that's why he didn't tell anyone he was sick?"

She nodded once, sharp. "He didn't want anyone to worry. Didn't want to feel pitied. It just made us angry, and God help me, that was worse than the grief for a while. I hated being angry at that boy. Do you know why I was angry, Ezra? Why we were all so mad at him?"

"Because he didn't tell you—"

"Because he was *selfish*. The one damn time in his life, and it was right there at the end." Her words were bitter and hot with anger, with something else that felt green-black and slimy. "He robbed us of a chance to say goodbye. To… to tell him we loved him. Because he didn't want to feel bad." She shot to her feet, waving me off when I reached out a hand towards her. "Just gimme a minute," she muttered, heading for the bathroom, the door wheezing shut behind her doing nothing to help her dramatic departure.

The room was quiet save for the muted sounds of closing credits and water running.

I wasn't being selfish by keeping this from Harrison or downplaying it with Oscar, who for all I knew still thought this was just a simple scan to see if I had epilepsy or something.

I wasn't.

I was keeping Oscar from losing his damn mind.

I was making sure Harrison didn't screw up his career just to be bored at my bedside.

My phone gave another angry buzz. I couldn't avoid him much longer.

Becky emerged from the bathroom, face damp and shining pink, in time to see me eyeballing my phone. "You should give him a call back before he comes down the wire and jumps out of that screen."

"That's… an image." I shoved the phone under my thigh, hiding it away in a fit of object permanence denialism. "It's late. He said he was going to bed."

She leveled a hard look at me. "Do you believe that, Ezra?"

A half-dozen responses popped to the tip of my tongue: flat denial, snide pushback, diversion (*tell me more about Ricky*), but what came out instead was, "I'm scared."

She blinked, momentarily startled from the look on her face, then she smiled, crossing to my side in just three short steps. Her hands cupped my face, tilting me up so I could see her gleaming eyes staring back at me. She was warm, which surprised me because it seemed like everything in a hospital should be frozen, and everyone who had touched me so far had been the temperature of a well digger's arse in February. Her expression hovered somewhere between exasperation and affection, stinging inside my chest.

So that's what a mum who didn't hate your guts felt like, I thought wildly.

Then, where the hell did that come from.

"If you weren't scared, you wouldn't be human," she said softly, barely above a whisper. "And I'm gonna tell you something I wish I'd told Ricky. You're doing no one any favors by trying to protect them from their own feelings. By trying to protect them from life and death."

She bent forward and pressed a smacking kiss to my forehead. "Now. You might be NPO till after your scan, but I'm not. I'm gonna go grab something bad for me from the cafeteria and we'll reconvene back here in twenty minutes to watch *Babylon A.D.*" She gave my cheek a pat and turned to let herself out of the room, throwing over her shoulder, "Call him."

"But what if he is mad?"

"Then he's mad." She paused and glanced back, halfway out of the room already. "That's how you know he still loves you."

CHAPTER 5

*I*t should come as no surprise to anyone who knows me that I did not call Harrison back right away.

Becky said twenty minutes, so I waited for fifteen. *If I have to, I can tell him my nurse just came in and I need to go,* I reasoned with myself.

Becky was right—I'm an arsehole.

Harrison answered on the first ring. Hell, he answered before the first ring finished.

"Hey," I drew out. "I need to say something and it's not… great."

Harrison inhaled slowly, that sort of reverse sigh he did whenever he was frustrated but trying not to be. "What've you gotten into?"

To his credit, he listened without interrupting. He was so quiet, in fact, I thought maybe he'd hung up on me or I'd dropped the call somehow. "Hello? Harry?"

"I'm on my way to the airport," he said flatly. "Do not fuck around with me on this, Ezra. I'm flying back right now, and I'm coming to the hospital."

"I'm—"

"If you say *fine*, we are going to have words, and you are not going to like most of them," he said. I could hear his teeth clenching, and I knew that the vein in his temple was likely doing some heavy lifting.

"Hey. Hey, breathe, baby. Remember what Doctor Eaman said about your blood pressure?"

"Ezra. I swear to god…"

My chest hurt. The machines were making angry noises at me, but so far no staff had come running to make sure I wasn't dying. Which was both a relief and kind of worrisome.

"It's… it's just a test," I whispered. "It's just a test, Harrison. I'm getting a scan in the morning, and I had some earlier today—well, I suppose I had them yesterday since it's after one a.m. now—and I have one more to do. But it's a big and fiddly one, so they decided to keep me in overnight since I was here anyway." *And just in case they saw something that couldn't wait.*

Harrison was quiet for a long time. His breathing slowed but grew no less irritated. "Ezra. I know you're not telling me everything. Don't," he interrupted when I started to protest, "don't start. Please. It used to make me upset, when you'd do this."

My heart ached, squeezing in protest of Harrison's words. "Harry…"

He swallowed audibly, and I wished I was—cursed the fact I wasn't—there to hold him, to tell him I was sorry and this had seemed like a good idea at the time, that I loved him too and that he was right, this was a mistake.

"It used to make me upset," he repeated more firmly. "But I know now that when you do this, you're scared. And I can't make whatever is scaring you go away, but I can be there for you if you let me. And baby, I want you to let me. I love you, Ezra, and sometimes I don't think you believe that."

"I love you too," I whispered finally. "I love you so much Harrison. That's why… That's why…" My words died, thick and heavy in my throat.

Harrison sighed and started to say something, but it morphed into a swear. "Shit. We're here. I need to pay the driver, okay? I'll be in Houston by seven. Don't fucking go anywhere, understand me?"

"Visiting hours start at nine," I murmured. "But I'll be getting my scan by then."

"They have waiting rooms, don't they?" he muttered dryly. "Just… wait for me, okay?"

I nodded, even though he couldn't see me. "I love you."

"Then please, Ezra… Please act like it."

BECKY TOOK HER TIME RETURNING. "I thought you said twenty minutes," I muttered when she sauntered in half an hour after she'd left.

"I wanted to give you time to talk to your fella." She smiled, returning to her post on the sofa. "How's he doing?"

Becky listened with a bland expression as I told her how Harrison had found out where I was, how hurt he'd sounded. When I wound down, she reached out to pat the back of my hand with the IV in it, making an apologetic face when I winced. "Well, now, it sounds to me like your careful little plan went to shit, huh?"

"Oh my god," I groaned. "So much shit. Oscar and Julian are cutting their trip short just to sit in the waiting room—Hell, I'll be done and out of here before they even get to the hospital! And I'm willing to bet CeCe is the one getting Harrison from the airport." I blew out an exasperated, embarrassed breath. "The waiting room is going to be chaos in a few hours."

She settled back, pulling a blanket over her legs and taking up the remote again. "Well, let's hope that you're in your scan and well underway before the troops arrive. I don't want to have to sign any witness statements."

I dozed for most of *Babylon A.D.,* but to be fair I think most audiences did (even Becky seemed less than enthused about Vin in this one). A loud and flashy sequence dragged me out of my drowse to stare in some confusion at the screen. "You know, when we first started filming the show for UnReality, there was this little old lady who loved Vin Diesel who helped Oscar get back to the house we'd been filming at."

She raised a brow. "I'm neither little nor old," she reminded me dryly.

"Never said you were. Just that this," I waved my hand at the screen, "is making me think of her. Of then."

"Tell me about it." She yawned, barely managing to stifle it behind her hand. "I've seen all the episodes y'all have out, but I don't remember any old broad trying to be too fast or too furious."

I rambled for a bit then, about the first episode we made for the channel, about how Oscar and I started making little videos for social media long before then. About… Hell, about a lot of things. By the time Vin had wrapped up his sci-fi venture, Becky was ready to murder my parents for me and also in possession of far too much information about Julian's quirks and peccadilloes.

"Julian sounds like another one of your people," she noted. "It doesn't come through much on the show, but you're not in front of the camera very much, are you?"

"I like filming." I shrugged. "And the technical bits and bobs. I'm good at it, and it makes my brain feel less like hopped-up squirrels at a rave than most other things."

She snorted again. "Ricky said his brain was like a hamster on a coke bender."

"ADHD powers, activate. Live, laugh, lisdexamfetamine."

She shook her head, smiling ruefully. "I wish you could've met him somehow. You two… two peas in a pod, I think. Well. Maybe in another life."

"Maybe," I said slowly. "Earlier, you said you weren't sure if you believed or not."

"That wasn't a question," she noted, muting the next movie so that Richard B. Riddick woke in silence on the screen.

"I've always believed," I admitted. "Nothing big ever made me say oh yeah, ghosts are totally real, how did I never know before. I just… did. And when I was seven, I realized I could feel them. I told my mum, and that's when I started my frequent visits to Her Majesty's Grippy Sock Vacation Homes."

Becky was quiet, watching me with something soft in her gaze. It made me squirm, fidgeting with the bandage holding the needle in my hand until she gently pushed my fingers away. "You told me that earlier," she reminded me gently. "About your parents sending you to the mental hospitals."

"Not so much sending me as *allowing me to be sent*. But yeah. I think that's the part that got to them more than me believing in ghosts. The fact I was feeling their feelings, able to tell things about them. They got scared, I think, and worried I'd do that to them. Or maybe they really did think the Devil had gotten to me. My family is very… let's say fond of particularly niche theological theories."

"Hon, I live under the buckle of the Bible belt. I know the sort."

"Well. Cheers then. But the thing was, it didn't occur to me that believing in ghosts was somehow weird until someone told me it was. Well. Several someones. A right talking-to along with a hypodermic of antipsychotic meds."

The memory brought with it the sharp, sweet, chlorine taste of the injection, my mouth flooding with it the same as it did after every shot they gave me. I grabbed the cup of water on the bedside table, gulping in hopes of washing the taste off, swallowing down the memory before it lodged itself right between my eyes to haunt me again.

Becky waited for me to calm a bit before asking, "And why do you think it's important whether or not I believe?"

I shook my head and fiddled with that damn sheet again. Because it's a safety check. It's making sure you're not going to tell the doctor who oversees my diagnosis that I'm talking to people who aren't there, that I'm living in a dreamworld. Maladaptive is what they told my parents. Maladaptive coping mechanisms. And I want to know if you believe me or if you're laughing at me when you leave the room.

"Most of the people I meet these days believe. That's why I meet them. The handful who don't aren't kind about it. Think we're con artists or crazy or both. And… I just suppose… I'm wondering if you get comfort from believing Ricky could still be around in a real way. If the possibility that he's a ghost is, I don't know… helpful? Peaceful?"

When she spoke next, she was blunt as hell, startling me out of my impending spiral. "You're wondering what will happen when you die. If the people you're leaving behind will get any sort of comfort from the idea of you, or if you get to be a spook, from your spirit lingering."

"I…"

She raised a brow, waiting.

"Yeah." I sighed. "Yeah, I am. I've experienced literally hundreds of hauntings—just the ones I know of for sure—since the age of seven. Maybe more, if I didn't realize that what I was feeling belonged to a ghost and not the living."

"How many of them were happy being ghosts?"

"I have no idea. Oscar might know. Some were happy enough, but it wasn't so much to do with being ghosts as seeing their loved ones thrive, or just existing in a loop of a very good day they'd had —those ghosts never realized we were there," I added. "Just caught in their feedback loop of existence until they wear out, I suppose."

I paused, taking a shaking breath and closing my eyes. Exhaustion nibbled at the edges of everything, but I couldn't bring myself to give in, to sleep. If I fell asleep, I'd dream, and I didn't want to dream of anything right then.

"Some ghosts, they weren't happy at all. They were angry they were dead. Or sad. Most were resigned to it, like they knew there was little choice in the matter. Julian's been trying to study that, if ghosts have any choice in becoming a ghost, why some people do and others don't..." I trailed off. "Well. All that to say, some are happier than others. Just like the living."

"Does it correlate with how they were in life? Like an angry person is an angry ghost?"

"Sometimes. Some ghosts we've met were right arseholes in life —not the charming kind, either—and carried on after death." I smirked. "I'm going to be a charming ghost."

She ignored that, pressing onward. "And the kind ones? The ones so full of love and care that it just spilled out of them when they smiled?"

A few, a very few, had felt like that. Golden sunrise glowing peace and joy, a happiness I hadn't felt with the living before. But they had been dead when I felt that. I had no idea what they were like when they were alive. I just shook my head, shrugged. She made a thoughtful sound in her throat, watching me intently in the dim light from the car park.

"Now the ten-million-dollar question. What kind of ghost would you be, Ezra Baxter?"

"Ah..." The kind who didn't want to be one. The kind who wasn't ready to be one. Who felt guilty for being one because it meant he'd disappointed his loved ones. *Again.*

"The kind that was so full of upset, he carries it on with him into the next world? Or maybe caught in that loop thingy, just reliving a moment over and over again? Or an angry one, mad at the world he left behind?" She turned up the volume a bit— Riddick was really hitting his stride, dramaturgically speaking. "Maybe a guilty one like in the stories, hm? Pacing and wailing, feeling bad for something they did in life?"

"What kind do you think I'd be?"

She shook her head. "You tell me."

After several minutes, she added, "Ricky would be one of those ghosts that moves furniture around, if he could. One of the ones that sticks by their loved ones just in case they need help, even though he'd be beyond being able to help us. Which would make him frustrated. So, he'd spend eternity, if he's a ghost, annoyed with the world and feeling useless."

"Is that the kind of ghost you think I'd be, then? I think I might be insulted."

She shrugged one shoulder, not looking away from the screen. "You tell me. If you dropped dead tomorrow, what would keep you here, Ezra Baxter? Guilt? Anger? Love?"

We watched the movie in silence for a long time. After a bit, I noticed Becky was drowsing, head pillowed on one hand, trying to stay upright. "Go to sleep," I muttered. "You need it."

She cracked one eye, giving me a gimlet glare. "You'd make a terrible ghost, Ezra, because you're not nearly done living yet."

CHAPTER 6

$\mathcal{B}$ecky was still there when an aide came to take my vitals just before dawn. He nodded to her sleeping form on the sofa and smiled. "She's like the floor mom," he whispered.

"She does this a lot?"

"Not a lot. Just… when it's needed," he murmured, making notes on the tablet about my readings, and humidity, and barometric pressure, and who knows what else. "Becky's got a huge heart. If she's hanging out with you, dude, that means you must need the friend."

"I have friends," I protested weakly. "It's not even visiting hours yet. Just wait, this place will be neck deep in people who want to crawl up my ass about underplaying the severity of this situation."

He shot me a bemused look as he checked my IV line. "Weirdo. But hey, do you." He fiddled with the heart monitor leads, making more notes, then paused, nibbling on his upper lip for a second as he darted a glance at me from below his lashes.

"Yeah, I'm on that show," I said, knowing that look well.

"I know. I'm just wondering if, um…" His tan cheeks darkened with a blush, and he refused to meet my gaze, instead becoming very focused on his tablet. "Do you know if there's anyone, you know, *here?*"

My knee-jerk reaction was to be an ass, to be snarky and say *yeah, us!* Or tell him to ask Oscar since I'm not much use when it comes to things like that, not unless I let my guard down.

You'd make a terrible ghost.

"Is there anyone you're hoping for?" I asked gently. "Someone you knew?"

He shrugged. "There's a lot of people who come through, you know? Some just sort of stick with you when they're gone, one way or another."

"And you're hoping someone stuck around?"

He sighed, blowing out his cheeks and finally lifting his gaze to mine. "I don't know. If they're still around, even just sticking their head in, so to speak, it'd be nice, you know? Maybe miss them a little less. But then I'd worry they were stuck. I mean, who wants to be in a hospital for eternity?"

"I... can't say for sure," I said delicately. "But that old chestnut about *they're always in your heart?* That's true. I mean, it's not the same. And it sucks. But they are there. And, well," I added before his disappointed expression could droop any lower, "I've been around a *lot* of hauntings, and my bestie is pretty much the best medium in the world—don't tell him I said that or he'll get a big head. There've been a lot of ghosts who stuck around for one reason or another, and just knowing someone remembered them made them happy. I mean, they weren't thrilled with being dead, but..." I trailed off. "I'm sorry. I wish I could help you more."

He shook his head, eyes bright and smile tight. "It's okay. I don't know if I'd want them to be here, really. But I was thinking earlier, after seeing your name on the roster for tonight, and thought I'd ask."

"Hey," I called softly before he could shut the door behind him. "If they were here, what would you say?"

He hesitated, a complicated series of expressions crossing his face. Finally, he sighed again. "I'd tell her I love her. And I miss her so much. And I'm so fucking mad at her for deciding to… to make an early exit. Because I'm selfish, and we were supposed to grow old together and sit on a porch somewhere, and make fun of people jogging by while we drank margs and shared a bowl. But she didn't wait. Couldn't, I guess." He shook his head, sniffing and straightening up from his slouch. "Sorry, that was highly inappropriate. I apologize."

His words had been a rush, breathless and tinged with a barely restrained sob. And worse, they'd hit me square in the chest and burrowed inside. *Would that be Harrison? Oscar? Would they be telling a stranger about my death because I decided it was better to keep this to myself?*

"I know it won't make it easier, but I think… No, I'm sure that a lot of the times when life is too hard for someone, it's not because of something we did as their friend. That… whatever you're worried about not having done, it wasn't that."

He nodded, turning his shining eyes away to fiddle with the whiteboard, erasing a corner of the E in my name and redrawing it while he sniffed. "Sorry," he muttered. "That was inappropriate."

"It's fine," I promised quietly. "I won't tell a soul."

He smiled a little less painfully and shrugged. "Your test is in a few hours. Try to get some rest."

Becky snuffled in her sleep, explosion-filled action sequences winging her to dreamland. And I was alone. For all intents and purposes. Alone with a thousand reminders that whatever was happening to me, it wouldn't be just on me. I wouldn't be going into this alone. And while I might have protested to anyone who'd listen, deep inside me where I hid all of the things I wasn't allowed to know, wasn't allowed to feel for years, didn't *want* to feel… Deep down in that spot I kept the tiny sliver of relief, of *happiness*, that I wouldn't be alone.

And the dragon of guilt that roared to life at that acknowledgment was heavy.

As if summoned by that flicker of relief that woke the guilt, my phone buzzed to show me a call from Oscar I'd managed to just miss thanks to my ringer being turned all the way down. "Shit, shit, shit…" I dialed him back before he could try again.

Oscar answered on the second ring. "I'm in the lobby," he announced. "They won't let me up. Tell them to let me up!"

"Sorry, you must have the wrong number. I don't know who this is."

"Ezra Jolene Baxter!"

I laughed. "As awesome as I am, I can't control the hospital's visiting hours or security team."

"Excuse me, ma'am?" Oscar said sharply. "My best friend and platonic soulmate is upstairs about to go into a PET test later this morning, and I've just flown all the way from England to… Yes. No? I'm sorry, what did you just say to me?"

I burst into a cackling laugh that I'm sure disturbed at least a few people on the floor. "Oscar, you posh git!"

"Shut up," he muttered. "I heard from Harrison. Seriously, Ezzy? He found out from CeCe?" Oscar tutted. "I'll murder you later. And then raise you from the dead and yell at you when you're unable to escape because I'm going to have Julian give me some of that weird stone stuff they used to make that ghost trap, and I'll keep you in a little ghost cage to shout at you until *I* die, then you won't be able to escape me ever."

Distantly, I heard Julian's bemused, *Love you too, Oscar.*

Oscar muffled the phone but not very well. "Oh, hush. You know I'm haunting the hell out of you if I go first. Don't be jealous."

"Ozzy—"

"No. No, no, no, no! No. I'm so disappointed right now, Ezra, but I love your stupid arse, and I'm not going to yell at you in a hospital bed, understood? But you *have* to talk to Harrison later. He… he's hurting. And I know that's a shit thing to lay at your feet right now, but it's the truth."

I nodded, unable to form words. And Oscar knew because he made a small, satisfied noise before muffling the phone again. "We won't even bother anyone else," Oscar stated to whomever was there with them.

Julian said something in return, and suddenly there was a scuffling sound and Oscar snapping *Oi! Watch the hands!*

"Oscar, what's going on?" I demanded. "Talk to me!"

"Security is asking us to leave because apparently I've made a scene and I'm allegedly disturbing people. There's no one up here but me and Julian," he added.

Becky's quiet voice cut in. "I'll go down and talk to them," she promised. "Need to get up to pee anyway. And I'll let 'em know when they can come back." She winked at me, struggling up from the sofa. "Oh, God, I'm old. I'll go work my magic on the front desk and security folks, get 'em to be sweet when your boyfriend and his fella come back later. Alright?"

"I heard her," Oscar said. "I must admit, I'm surprised Ezra. You having a woman in your room."

"Well. I always said I'd sleep with a woman over my dead body."

Oscar snorted, then choked. "Not funny, arsehole."

"Oh, it's funny. You're just on a time delay with the humor."

He was quiet for a long moment, Julian's low murmur as he spoke with someone—security, likely—the only sound on the line until Oscar sighed anew. "I love you, wanker. Don't die before I see you again. Do you promise?"

"I… I'll do my best."

"Prat," he whispered.

"Bellend."

After a beat, he hung up.

Better that way, I thought. We often did that because we both hated saying goodbye. It was better to leave a conversation unfinished, open-ended. Even on an insult. Because that meant you were coming back.

It was childish—which made sense because we started doing

that when we were twelve—but it was *ours,* and for two codependent trauma monkeys like us, it worked.

Until it didn't.

Because it wasn't going to work with me maybe dropping dead, something eating away at my brain. Something I knew Oscar and Harrison (and Julian and CeCe) were going to get on my arse about because I'd avoided any sort of EKG, CT, or other scan for so long. Afraid of what they'd see in there, since my seizures started.

Afraid it meant something bad.

And here we are. Something Bad Central.

Becky had slipped out while I was still talking to Oscar, and I was finally truly alone in my room.

With my thoughts.

Goddamnit.

It was barely seven in the morning, too early for me to be up. At least by my standards. My party days were long behind me though, and I knew I wouldn't be able to get to sleep at this point, with the sun up. Though, to be fair, I hadn't really had party days so much as *staying up playing TTRPGs with Oscar and whoever else we could rook into it while drinking wine coolers and pretending we were cool.*

Fuck, I was exhausted. Scrubbing my hands over my face, I eyeballed the bathroom, wondering if I could make it there and back without having to drag half the telemetry department with me.

Reluctantly, I pressed the call button. Someone came on over the tiny intercom built into the bed and asked if it was an emergency. "Nah, I just need to go to the lav."

A pause, then, "Someone will be there shortly. Just sit tight for a minute."

A minute passed. Then two. Then three.

My bladder, never one to tell time, informed me that any longer and I'd become a fountain.

Fuck this, I decided, swinging my legs over the edge of the bed, wincing as my feet hit the cold floor. My lovely backless gown flapped in the breeze when I pushed to my feet, wobbling a little thanks to low blood sugar and being on my back for so many hours.

When I'd gotten some cold water on my face, filled my fancy giant hospital travel mug they'd plopped on my bedside table, had a piss… I'd call Oscar and see if they were still downstairs. And then I'd beg Becky to take me down to see them, just for a few minutes. Because it was better to face the music, wasn't it?

And maybe… Fuck. Maybe take everyone's advice and stop shoving my head up my own bum when it came to needing help. To wanting support.

To let the shrieking little boy inside who wanted to be loved, damn it just… be loved.

Ugh. I'd turned into a fucking greeting card or some shit, and my bladder was fucking screaming. Enough dilly dallying.

I winced as a spike of pain shot down my neck and seemed to bloom up the base of my skull at the same time. A sharp, metallic smell hit me square in the face, making me gag. "What the fuck," I gasped.

Only it came out wrong.

Sound, not words.

"Shit. Help. Help!"

I swayed, pain beyond anything I ever imagined exploding now, blinding me. I was distantly aware of falling, bouncing off the side of the bed as I tried to sit and miss. The damn machines that had been such a pain to deal with finally, finally screaming to life.

CHAPTER 7

I dreamed of forgotten things, old memories stored deep in my head that were small and dusty, tucked away by childhood, wrapped in orange and brown and green with threads of pink and yellow tying them together. The faint pulse of pain behind my forehead danced along with my thoughts, punctuating everything with fist-pounding awareness that what I was seeing wasn't real. At least not anymore.

Cold seeped through the thin sheet tucked tight around my hips and legs, pulling me out of la-la land. Becky stood near the whiteboard, her frown deep and distracted as several people in scrubs leaned over me, talking in voices too tangled together for me to understand. "His eyes are open. Mr. Baxter," one of them said, voice loud and even, "follow my finger."

I tried. I don't know what I did though because the man frowned and disappeared from my line of sight. "Is the OR ready?"

"OR?" My voice was an atonal slur of sound. "OR?!"

Everything sort of smeared into a blur then. Becky's face replaced the man's, her plum-dyed ringlets bouncing as she jogged alongside the gurney. "Remember what I said? You'd be a terrible ghost?" Her smile was forced as she glanced down the corridor. "Hang tight, kid. We've got about a dozen more Vin Diesel movies to get through, got it?"

"Rather not," I mumbled, but I doubted she heard me.

Hell, I barely had.

"Hey. Hey, open your eyes, dipshit."

"Oh, Jesus, Mary, and Joseph. This had better not be the afterlife."

The man standing next to me—scruffy, tired-eyed, and smiling, shook his head. "Nah. Nothing *after* about it. You're still alive. Just a little busy right now." He nodded to something behind me, the bright light of the room leaching out to something less eye-searing as I turned to see a group of gown-clad people moving like ants around someone on a table.

Oh, who am I kidding? I knew immediately it was me. None of that *oh my god who could it be? Gasp, shock, horror, it can't be!* mess.

"Let me guess. Guardian angel?" I snarked. "Are you about to tell me I had a wonderful life and get your wings?"

"Oh, fuck that noise." He laughed. "Nah, that's for people like my grandma. She likes to think everything can be smoothed over and shiny and sparkly in the afterlife or heaven or whatever. My mom and I know better, though."

The realization was sharp and, frankly, awkward. "I should've known it was you right away, Ricky." I sighed. "You've got your mum's eyes."

"Why should you have known? Not like we've met before."

"Nah, but that's how these things work, right?" I watched the people moving over me with a soft sort of detachment. Part of me, deep down, was absolutely freaking the fuck out. But it was like watching a movie on one of those old telly screens while I peered through a window with a mesh curtain in the way. "The dead are never far off—something I learned a long time ago. And I'm guessing you were 'round your mum. Saw an opportunity and jumped in." I glanced at him. "What're you giving me that look for?"

"Wondering what it's like to live in such a simple mind." He sighed, shaking his head. "Must be nice."

"Oi, fuck off then. No one invited you to my death."

"You're not dying, dumbass. You're just… skating real close."

The sounds of the surgery were muffled by whatever you wanted to call it: the veil, the divide, the light. Voices snapped and rushed, words indistinct but carrying urgency on their backs. "I think this hurts," I said softly. "Part of me feels it. Ghost pain." I snorted softly, repeating the words with different emphasis. "But I'm not dying? How do you know that?"

"I just do." He shrugged. "I've been hanging around Ma enough to see the signs and know what's what. That," he pointed at my body, "you've got a motherfucker of an aneurysm that ruptured, dude. If you'd been anywhere else, you'd be dead by now. As it is, you're gonna have a bitch of a road ahead." He tapped his forehead, giving me a small smirk. "Ask how I know."

"That kill you, then? An aneurysm? What about my tumor?"

"Can't tell you shit about a tumor, man. But aneurysms? Yeah, I can tell you all about those. It wasn't the cancer that got me. It was one of those assholes."

Something happened on the table. A doctor held her hands up and stepped back as blood spurted.

"Well, that ain't good," Ricky muttered. "Here we go."

The activity around my body took on a frantic but controlled vibe. I knew part of me was afraid, but the bits I was most immediately aware of? They were tired. Maybe a little curious. Subdued, more than anything. "When did you die?"

His brows arched in an expression like his mother's. "1999. Kind of rude to ask, by the way."

"It's not rude if you're trying to help," I muttered. "And Jesus, you've been here a bit, haven't you? Why the hospital?"

"Why not? Ma's here most of the time so…" He trailed off, watching the people move around the table. It had a rhythm to it, their movements, a comforting assuredness that made me think that, even if Ricky was wrong and I went absolutely toes up today, they really had done all they could and maybe it was just my time.

"You miss her."

He nodded. "Of course I do. I'm dead. I can spend all the time I want with her, and sometimes, she knows I'm there, but it's not the same. I can't show up after a shitty date and have a cup of coffee with her, complain about men together. I can't go over at Thanksgiving or Christmas and fucking have cookies or help make a goddamn pie! And you know what sucks the most?"

"The being dead part?"

"Ass. I mean, you're not wrong, but you didn't have to say it aloud. But what sucks just as much is the fact I robbed her of minutes. Of just a few stupid fucking minutes because I didn't want to see her upset. Because I didn't want to need help."

"So, this isn't about a wonderful life but still a cautionary tale?"

"It's something." He sighed, scrubbing his hands through his hair. I wondered if he felt it or if it was just a remembered habit. I'd never thought to ask Oscar about that, and it seemed a bit rude to ask Ricky right now, all things considered.

"I'm not here to guilt you into anything but just… I get it, okay? And this?" He pointed at my body again. "This isn't something you can just shake off. Let them help you. Let yourself be miserable. Don't think you have to always be *on*. Don't do this alone. We all die alone, even surrounded by people, but I died *alone*. Ma didn't find out for hours. She had no idea I was even going in for surgery. And for almost a quarter of a fucking century now, you know what she does? Kicks herself for it," he said before I could even guess an answer (for the record, that was going to be my guess).

"If I wake up—"

"You will. Doctor Morley's great. I've seen her do some amazing shit with brains, man. Wish she'd been here when I had my little," he paused and made a popping sound with his lips. "The other guy? Dude was all thumbs."

I went on as if he hadn't spoken. "Want me to tell your mum you said hey, then? That you miss her?"

He shook his head, a small and sad little jerk of his chin. "She knows. Hell, she's my mom, you know? How can she not? And I don't miss her like you think. It's not like that when you're dead. It's... it's more frustrating. Because I can spend an entire day by her side, never leaving her for one second, but she doesn't hear me. Or see me. Not usually. And when she does, it's this whole thing, you know? And that just kind of makes it worse. The sobbing. Spending the next day in bed, holding the old stuffed elephant I got as a baby. If I was still alive, I'd miss her in a normal way. It'd hurt, and be sad, but I'd know it was fixable. Hell, when she dies, I don't even know if we'll be in the same place, you know? What if she gets the express elevator to heaven as a reward for years of putting up with so much bullshit and I'm still here at the hospital, moping around? Or kicking around her place in Sugarland, waiting for someone to tell me the secret code to get in the pearly gates with my shitty track record?

"I don't think that's how it works. But I'm really the wrong person to say. All I do is get the vibes, you know? Empathy. Works better with the dead than the living for me, but Oscar... He's the one you need to talk to."

"Is he though?" He shifted, putting himself between me and the table. My body. "I think maybe it's you. Because he's not the one I see here trying to be a stoic asshole and refusing to let his friends in. And that old dude you're all moony eyed over."

"Hey! Harrison's not old!"

"Dude's at least thirty-five, man."

Thirty-eight. "Still not old."

"Whatever. Why aren't you stressing about him, man? It's waah waah waah Oscar this and Oscar that, like he's all that and a bag of chips. But where's the love for Gramps?"

"He knows. He's on his way here."

"You told him?"

I hesitated, but Ricky waited me out. "He found out by accident. I was going to tell him after the PET scan, but someone beat me to it."

Ricky sucked his teeth. "Dick move, man. Once your head's healed up, you're gonna have a lot of kissing ass to do."

We watched them work on me for a little while—maybe a minute? Maybe more. The doctor who seemed to be in charge of the procedure was doing something with a tube, moving some bit of computerized equipment with a tiny joystick thing. I felt the ghost of it in my skull, the faintest sensation of movement, of *not right* happening somewhere in all that gray matter.

"So why are you here, then? Bored?" I finally asked. "We're not doing some Dickens shite, you're not here to teach me some lesson or help me cross over so… Why are you here?"

"Am I though?"

"Oh, Christ."

Ricky laughed softly. "You don't know, though, do you? Maybe I'm a figment of your imagination. You'll forget me when the anesthesia wears off. Or maybe I'm a product of brain damage from the rupture." His expression was sly and calculating when he added, "Maybe I'm here because of your seizures. How long have they thought you might have had a tumor? Maybe I've been lurking in there the entire time. I'm just the product of your brain going haywire right now."

"You're a shitty doom-bringer," I muttered.

"Or maybe," he went on, ignoring me. "Maybe I'm really here. And I'm really the ghost of a dead guy who never got to live and spent most of his life trying to keep everyone around him happy and safe."

The sound of suction, of metal on soft things, broke through my haze. "Maybe," I conceded. "Or maybe you're just here to be a dick and you're not Becky's son at all." Not that I could blame him if that was the case—I'd probably do the same if I got bored after I died.

His smile was positively pretty, and I felt a sharp pang over the fact I'd never get to talk to him later. The envy I thought I'd lost over Oscar's abilities roared back to life, and I wanted to cry about how unfair it was. Ricky was never going to get to hang out with anyone again, never get to get a beer with friends. Never get to argue with someone face-to-face and make up later.

He'd never get to grow old with someone, if he wanted.

Harrison…

"Stop looking so sad," he grumbled. "Seriously. I already feel like crap being dead and all. You being all mopey isn't helping."

"And that's why I didn't want to say anything about what's going on."

Ricky sniffed delicately, smoothing his hands over the worn-soft T-shirt he wore forever before glancing back at me. "Not the same, dipshit."

"You already called me that."

"If it ain't broke…"

Something jerked low in my neck, sending a dull thrum of pain through my skull.

"You're not alone, Ezra. You're not the person you kept telling yourself you had to be, and that's not a bad thing. Your friends, your grandpa-boyfriend? They love your stupid ass. And what you need to get through that thick skull—ha—is the fact you're allowed to ask for help. To admit you're scared. You're not some fucking monolith, okay?" He flicked his fingers at me like he was flicking a cigarette. He made a face at his hands, shaking his head. "God, I miss smoking. Fuck."

"Well, if there's ever a good time to take up a lethal habit, post-mortem is it."

He snorted, eyes crinkling like his mum's. "Dark humor. Nice. I like you."

"Consider me flattered."

"Look, they're gonna be wrapping up sooner rather than later, and chances are you won't remember a goddamn thing I've said. At least not clearly. So, if nothing else, remember this. Ezra Baxter, you'd make a terrible ghost."

"Your mum said the same thing," I murmured. "Weird."

"Is it though? Or is it a product of your scrambled brain feeding you bits and pieces of memory while they install the new deck and in-ground pool up in that noggin of yours?" He leaned closer and, for just a moment, I smelled warm skin and aftershave and coffee with a hint of cigarette smoke under it all. A ghost perfume, gone before I could really enjoy it, before I could name all the parts and instead just trailed after it when he smirked up at me and whispered, "Either way, Ezra, you know in your heart of hearts that I'm right. So, when you get up and out of here, remember you'd be a terrible ghost, and if you want to be a better one, you gotta stop making dumbass choices. No one wants to be haunted by the ghost of angsty emo boyfriends past."

"There's an entire generation of My Chemical Romance fans who'd beg to differ."

"Huh?"

"Sorry, let me put that in nineties speak for you. An entire generation of Pearl Jam fans."

"Shit for brains," he muttered. "Pearl Jam sucks." The voices in the room grew louder, faster. Not frantic, just determined and sure. "Here we go," he cheered, turning to me with a wide grin. "I changed my mind. Say hi to my mom, okay? If you remember. Tell her… Tell her she was hella wrong about Grandma's dog. That little demon is definitely in hell."

I sputtered a laugh, something behind my navel tugging hard until I was falling, then swimming in the dark.

Then everything was heavy and painful, and I couldn't make any sounds beyond a moan, but that was okay because that was the only sound I wanted to make.

CHAPTER 8

"Now what do we do when we're having health problems?" CeCe asked primly, waving her finger around as if presiding over a crowded lecture. "Ah, yes, you in the front. Mr.… Weems, is it?"

"Doctor Weems."

"If you say so."

Julian stuck out his tongue at his sister before answering in just as prim of a tone, "You tell the people who love you."

"Very good! Have a treat." She tossed him a peanut M&M, which he snagged out of the air and popped in his mouth. "Okay, next question—"

"Alright, alright," I groaned. "I know, I'm an arse. Can we get to the part where you all hate me for a while?"

Ever since I'd woken up in the ICU after surgery to successfully repair the ruptured aneurysm (so yay, not a tumor! But boo, aneurysm!), Oscar's pale, scruffy face leaning over mine, I'd been on tenterhooks, waiting for the shouting, the tears.

Well, the angry tears.

What I'd gotten was… Goddamn it. Love and support.

"Dumbass," Julian muttered. "We don't hate you. We're worried about you."

"Next question," CeCe repeated. "What do we do when someone we love makes a dumbass decision like trying to downplay the seriousness of their health condition?"

"Oh, I know!" Julian said eagerly, raising his hand again. "We call them on it!"

"Good job! Here, have another."

This time, he leaned back and caught it in his mouth.

"I say this with the utmost love and respect," I muttered. "Fuck both of you."

CeCe grinned, popping an M&M into her own mouth then. "I'll save the lightning round for when Oscar gets back with lunch."

They'd forced him and Harrison to go home, shower, and come back with takeaway. Both of them were fairly scruffy and ripe when I finally came 'round enough to recognize faces consistently, and they hadn't gotten better in the intervening days. Julian and CeCe had done the creepy twin telepathy thing, and in some sort of choreographed maneuver, gotten them both out the door of my room and down the hall past the nurse station before they realized what was happening.

Which left me with the Wonderful Weems Twins and their giant bag of candy as CeCe played gameshow host and not so subtly razzed me for my choices.

Julian settled back in the chair beside the bed, eyeballing the telly. "What is with this hospital and Vin Diesel?"

CeCe joined him, sitting on the arm of the chair, but instead of watching whatever car movie was playing, she reached out and very gently touched the part of my head that'd been shaved for surgery. "You know, if you grew this out a little, and left the other side long, it could be a look."

"Maybe I'll get a zipper tat over the scar," I suggested, wiggling my brows at her. "Or a pull tab."

CeCe pursed her lips thoughtfully. "Nah, get the production company logo. I'll give you a hell of a bonus."

"No shit?"

She grinned. "One way to find out."

A nurse clattered in, pushing a cart of equipment ahead of her. "Hey, y'all, I need to get some vitals and do a few things with Mr. Baxter here, so if y'all don't mind stepping out for a minute?"

Julian and CeCe made some half-arse comments about checking out the cafeteria when we all knew they'd be lurking just outside the door like every other time someone had come in and asked guests to leave.

I kind of liked it. The guilt that came with that realization wasn't the dragon sitting on my chest this time. Just maybe… a hefty chuckwalla.

The nurse did her thing, then promised me the neurologist would be coming by during her rounds to make another assessment and they'd start the ball rolling on my release.

I hadn't seen Becky in a week. I thought about asking the nurse checking me over but decided not to.

Because I might be experiencing remarkable personal growth, but I was still a fucking coward.

Ricky had been wrong. I didn't forget anything.

Left alone again for a few minutes, I closed my eyes. The medications made everything feel a little fuzzy, a little too nice. When Harrison slipped into the room, I was riding the low-grade buzz of a possible nap. But I opened my eyes for him. Usually so put together, even on his days off, Harrison looked haggard now. Blue-gray circles under his eyes, three-day scruff on his cheeks and chin, an old t-shirt with some marathon logo from years ago fading on the front… He was a shell of his usual put-together self, tendrils of deep yellow and brown and red tangling whenever he looked at me, anxiety coloring everything he felt. "You look like shit," I murmured with a small smile, holding out my non-IV hand towards him.

"Thanks, I feel like shit, so it's nice to have my effort appreciated." He kissed my cheek, smelling faintly of coffee and chips. "Oscar's flirting with a nurse, so I seized the moment to see you on my own."

"Oscar won't mind giving us time alone."

"Hence his flirting."

Harrison sank down to sit on the side of the bed, his fingers tangling with mine and holding on hard. Almost too hard. "I love you. And you hurt me deeply. Because you decided what was best for me instead of trusting me."

"What I did was… a bad choice," I said slowly. "I know we've discussed that. But—"

"But," Harrison cut me off. "Ezra, let me talk. Please."

"Okay."

He breathed out slowly, shakily. Then he was quiet. He stared at his hands where they were loosely folded on the side of my bed. He breathed—not hard like he was mad but just… breathing.

And said nothing.

"Harry?"

"The thing is, you confuse me."

Ouch.

He spread his fingers, brushing them against my wrist below the IV port. "Just when I think there're no more layers to get through, I find out there's one more. And sometimes I wonder if you'll ever stop trying to hide from me, Ezra." He looked up, pinning me with his implacable gaze. "I know you've been more yourself with me than with anyone else. Even Oscar sometimes."

I nodded slowly. We'd talked about it before, so late at night that it was early morning. There were things I couldn't share with Oscar, fears that he wouldn't understand.

Or maybe he would, but I'd just never let him…

Harrison's fingers wrapped around my wrist then, squeezing gently, so gently I could barely feel the pressure. "But then you pull that shell closed again. You hide from me and I… I get mad about

it. And sad. And I wonder if you truly want to be in this rela-
tionship."

"Harrison—"

"Let me finish."

Another nod. I was hot and cold, my throat working against an
icy lump of panic that threatened to strangle me. Harrison's
threads were dark—navy, plum, scarlet, black. But the faintest
trace of pale pale blue sparked through it—sorrow and loss,
holding the fear and anger and confusion and everything else
together.

"That isn't fair." He sighed. "It's not fair to either of us. And
what you did isn't fair either, Ezra. Do you understand?"

When I finally forced words past the ice, my voice was small
and scratchy. "Are you breaking up with me?"

When he didn't immediately say no, the ice shattered and
spread through my chest and belly. But Harrison finally shook his
head, tightening his grasp just a tiny bit more. "I thought about it.
But that… that also wouldn't be fair. Because I know you're not
doing this to be malicious. And I love you. And I want this to
work. So… I need you to talk to me, Ezra. If this is going to work,
there can't be more layers."

One more nod, slow and shaky.

He sighed through his nose, wilting just a little. "Okay. Now
you."

"I don't know if I can say anything more than I've said this
week. Not about this," I gestured to my head. "I thought… I
thought I was doing what was best for everyone. I didn't want you
all to walk on eggshells."

"Ezra, I love you so much it scares me sometimes. And I know
you love me. But you need to trust me. And yourself."

I stared for a long moment, trying to put together a response
that wasn't defensive. Because if there's one thing nearly dying had
taught me, it was some fucking self-awareness. Not much, but

some. "I've spent most of my life on the edges of things," I finally said, barely above a whisper.

"It's nothing you've done, Harry. I promise. And you don't make me feel excluded or second-best or any of that. It's," I paused, tapping my temple gently because god, did my entire fucking skull hurt, "it's my wiring, I think. I was a burden to my family until they decided I was a curse, a monster of some sort because I was too queer, too weird, too *me*. Then I drifted along after Oscar, like a baby duck." To be fair, though, Oscar was a baby duck too. But he handled leaving the nest better. "The idea of you, of Oscar, of anyone really but mostly the pair of you, having to care for me if I was… sick… Having to be dependent on you both when I know how hard it would be for you… And I'd become a burden. Something you resented. And I'd have to see that. And I'd have to watch you grieve before I died. And… And…" I took a deep and shuddering breath. "And I'd make a terrible ghost!"

"Ezra." He sighed, leaning carefully down beside me, half-laying on the bed and carefully, oh so carefully, touching my face, my hair, and the corner of my lips with his fingertips. "What the hell are you talking about?"

I couldn't help it. I snorted, and then I cried. Mostly from the ache in my head but also… not really. Harrison tensed—he was never good with crying—but pulled me a tiny bit closer and awkwardly, gently pat my back and shushed me like I was a child.

Which kind of made things worse for a few minutes until they got better.

"Oh god, I've got snot all over you."

"It's okay. I didn't go home to change in the first place, just sat in the parking lot and freaked out for an hour, so this is already dirty."

"Well, that's… good?"

He laughed softly, the sound small and low. "Ezra, I want you to go to a therapist."

"Wow. A guy nearly dies one time and suddenly he needs therapy?" Harrison tipped his head back to fix me with a look and I sighed. "I know, I know, I heard myself. But…"

"But?"

"But." I nodded and gingerly snuggled closer. "Okay. I'll… I'll see about it after I'm cleared to, you know, be among the living again."

A brisk, soft knock at the door had Harrison sitting up despite my plaintive *nooooo*. "Hey," Oscar said quietly. "How's the patient?"

"Alive," I replied, shifting to see him more clearly. "Hey."

He nodded. "Hey." A *look* passed between the pair of them, and Harrison slipped to his feet.

Crap.

"I'm going to go grab a coffee," he murmured. "Ezra, you want one? They said you were cleared for regular food so…"

"Ah. No coffee, but if they have an ice cream sandwich, I'd murder one."

Oscar held the door for him and in seconds, we were alone. "So, is today the day you've all decided I'm well enough to have serious conversations?" I asked.

"All of our conversations are serious," he rejoined, coming to sit on the bed beside me, far less ginger than Harrison had been but still careful.

"Even the ones about which Pokémon we could take in a fight?"

"Especially those. And I still say on my own, I'd be able to take down a Slowpoke, but if we were fighting together, at least a Tyrogue."

"Phhht. A Tyrogue would kick our ass. At best, we'd be able to take a Weepingbell. Just put a bucket over it."

Oscar rolled his eyes. This was an old thread for us, one we'd started soon after we'd met and one we bounced back to at least once a week. It was never serious, but it was a check-in. *I could absolutely take down a fighting style* meant we were in fine fettle. *Man, a Magicarp would kick my arse…* Well, that's the opposite, isn't it?

"What about you?" he asked, nudging me carefully. "Hand-to-hand combat. Which one?"

"Right now? Ugh. One of the little bug types. Whack 'em with my IV pole."

"That's not hand-to-hand," he reproved mildly, but there was a small smile at the corner of his lips, pressing in a dimple. "You'd have to use just your bare hands. No weaponry."

It felt good to have the silly-serious argument again. Normal. Right.

Except for the wary look in Oscar's eyes.

A nurse came and went again, this time with the promise of the doctor being there 'very soon'.

And by 'very soon' she meant 'right as she finished checking my healing wound' because Doctor Morley sailed in with her rainbow lanyard flying, bright green eyeshadow sparkling under the overhead lights, and looking altogether too happy and colorful to work in a ward full of people either recovering from almost dying or, well, dying.

"You must be Oscar," she announced, pointing at, well, Oscar. "I've met the partner—seriously, if he ever decides he's into the ladies, give him my number, oh my god I'm joking, I'm joking—and I've met the twins, but I keep missing you."

Oscar shifted a tad uncomfortably, his eyes wide as he took in the neurosurgeon who saved my sorry arse. "I'm... sorry?"

She laughed again, waving one hand airily. "Well, I figured I'd see you in the flesh before we cut Ezra loose here. Ezra, do you want Oscar to stay in here while we discuss what's what and how's that?"

"I don't mind if he doesn't."

Oscar raised his brows, his expression very carefully neutral. "I don't think I mind but I might revisit that statement if things get too gory."

She snorted at that. "You're healing well, all things considered, and you're not showing any indications of long-term neurological damage. The clip is permanent, and Doctor Creller, she's the neurologist on the team, I'm just the cutter," she added with a giggle, "is going to be prescribing several medications for you to take starting immediately, but we'll also be working with your GP and an endovascular specialist to determine if that's going to be long-term. The cause of your rupture is kind of a mystery right now. You said no family history?" she verified.

"Not as far as I know. But I've been estranged from those knobs for a while, so they might've all popped a vessel by now, for all I know." Or care.

She nodded, her expression falling into thoughtful lines for a moment before brightening again. "Well. We'll be running a few more scans this afternoon. Then," she snapped both fingers, "you're good to go."

"Today?" I struggled to sit up all the way, tangled in my IV line and the scratchy sheets. "No shit?"

"None whatsoever."

Oscar made a tiny *yay!* noise and leaned in to pull me into a hug as Doctor Morley laughed (I don't think she knew any other expression, though I had a memory of her sharp orders, a strident tone, barking at someone to *be effective,* but that might have been a dream). From there, everything kaleidescoped. Doctor Morley called for radiology to come and get me, Oscar scurried off to tell Julian, CeCe, and Harrison that I was being sprung, and I was suddenly in the middle of techs, aides, and nurses coming in to poke, prod, add IV lines and take others away, stick things to my chest and make me grateful I wasn't a very hairy sort of fellow, then scoot me into a wheelchair to whisk me away for another scan.

"You know," I muttered as the man pushing me down the brightly lit corridor headed for X-ray, "you'd think you'd want to expose me to *less* radiation, considering the whole cancer risk thing."

"It's how we stay in business," he said, smirking. "Gotta make you a repeat customer."

I snorted. And for the first time in weeks, I felt a tiny bit more normal than before.

AFTER THAT, it was stop-and-go for several hours. Tests didn't net instant results and had to be read by specialists, then Doctor Morley was in surgery, then, then, then…

CeCe and Julian went back to Harrison's and my place to make sure everything was ready. Harrison set up camp in the waiting room while I was taken for more scans, sent to give this fluid and that, and dosed with exciting new medications that would either help me or make me sick, or sometimes both.

And through it all, Oscar lurked like a ghost in the corner. Something I pointed out in a quiet moment between waves of people. "You're all Dickensian over there. Do you want to go grab some food or something?"

He shook his head. "I… I wasn't going to say anything. But earlier, much earlier, I heard what you said to Harrison. About being a terrible ghost. I was wondering what you meant by that."

"Ah. Becky told me I'd be a bad one," I chuckled weakly. I'd told Oscar all about her two days after surgery, when I was finally feeling less like death warmed over and more like just plain death. "And I think maybe she's right."

He huffed quietly. "I'd rather you not be a ghost at all. Not yet anyway."

"Me either."

He came closer, now that we were alone for a few minutes, and leaned his head against mine. "Ezzy, I was so fucking angry with you for a little while. But I want you to know that… that I get it. I think. And I'm still mad at you, but… I get it. And I meant it when I said I'd trap you in a ghost box thingy and make you stay there so I could yell at you if you died on me before we're very old."

"Oh, fuck, call the doctor back. My eyes are leaking."

"Fuck you," he said, though he was smiling. "You've never been a burden to the people who love you."

I nodded, unable to form words that weren't just a sob.

"Hey, do you think, before we go, we could track down Becky? I'm kind of surprised she hasn't been by yet." Surprised and a little hurt, to be honest.

Oscar glanced around, as if expecting her to leap out from behind my IV pole or crawl out from under the bed to surprise us. "Maybe it's her week off or something."

"Maybe…"

He kissed my forehead gently but with a smacking sound, making me snicker and call him granny lips. "I'll ask at the nurse's station."

"Hey… If I get mutant powers from all this radiation, what do you think about starting a YouTube channel about me being an anti-hero?"

He nodded thoughtfully. "Or, here's an idea… No."

"Oh, come on, it'll be fun!"

"That's what you said before we took that meeting with Jacob Grant and look where it got us."

I grinned, bumping my arm into his. "Yeah. Look at that."

CODA

*E*zra was downstairs somewhere, getting yet another picture of his brain and the metal clip holding the vessel closed. Julian and CeCe were gone—at Harrison and Ezra's place, making sure it was suitable for his recovery process. Harrison... Harrison was haunting the waiting room. He'd ostensibly been making calls, catching up on some work things, but he needed the time to break down, to be alone. He noticed me, seeing him with his face buried in his hands, cheeks wet and eyes red. He'd paused, giving me a small nod. And I understood. Nodding in return, I left him alone.

Out of the corner of my eye, I saw a man about my age stood at the end of the corridor, waiting. He noticed me and visibly startled, looking around as if to say *do you see this too?*

Ah... Of course.

I should've known.

The nurse's station was busy, a hive of organized chaos, so I gave it a wide berth for the time being, instead heading for the men's lav down the corridor to splash some cold water on my face.

The ghost followed me there. He was waiting behind me when

I lifted my face from my hands, still wet and cool. He waited as I dried off, checked the stalls, and then turned to him, spreading my hands wide. "How can I help you?"

"Ezra doing okay?"

Now it was my turn to startle. "How do you know Ezra?"

"Dude, everyone on this floor knows Ezra," he chuckled. "Living and dead. He's kind of a charming asshole when he wants to be."

"True." I smiled. "He's alright. They're releasing him today, if all goes well."

He nodded. "Good. Good. I told him the docs were awesome."

"No offense, but… Ezra *saw* you? He, um. He usually doesn't see ghosts."

"Not like you, huh?" the guy teased, smiling wryly. "Yeah, he seemed pretty down on himself about not being as good at that as you are." He raised one finger, silencing my incipient protest. "Though I don't think that's his real downer, you know? That's just what he latched onto."

I nodded. "Yeah. I know."

"I'm glad he's getting out of here. And I'm glad—Jesus, I'm fuckin' ecstatic—he's getting his head out of his ass. My mom… She's kind of not doing well since I popped my cork, you know? And I think she saw Ezra as too much like me."

A few pieces fell together with a click. "Your mum is Becky?"

He grinned. "Got it in one. She's awesome. And she deserved better than me, really. But here I am. Hanging out at my mom's job to…" He blew out a phantom breath. "I don't know, to be honest."

"Do you want to remain here?" I asked gently. "If you need help to cross, I can—"

"No," he said vehemently. "No. I'm staying as long as she is."

"Do you want to talk to her? I can help."

He hesitated. "I… maybe. Maybe so. She's, uh. She's not here today. They made her take some time off when she ended up crashing in Ezra's room the other night. They said it was inappropriate and yada yada yada." He rolled his eyes and looked impossibly young and alive for just a moment. "Look, I just wanted to check on Ezra, you know? Without my mom here it's harder for me to interact with stuff."

I nodded. "I understand."

He shifted, shoving his hands into his pockets, shuffling his feet. "I'll let you go. Just, um. If Ezra remembers me, tell him… tell him Ricky says hey. And keep his head out of his ass."

I nodded again. "I will. I promise. And, um. If you ever need help…"

He nodded. "I'll find you."

THREE DAYS after Ezra was home, two days after his first follow-up appointment, Ricky found me in my kitchen, drinking a cup of tea at two in the morning, unable to shake the image of Ezra's angry-looking scar, of how still he slept and what almost was.

"Hey."

"Shit!"

"Dude… That looks painful. Run some water over it!"

I glared, shoving my hand under the tap and turning the water to tepid. "Ricky. Hello."

"Hey, man. It was easier to find you than I thought. You're pretty famous on this side of things."

"So, I've heard."

He grinned, though his face fell into a sad sort of frown within a heartbeat. "Look, so, um, my mom was back at work today and, well. I think… I think it's time."

"For…?"

"Dude."

"Sorry, it's the middle of the night. I'm not fully functional at the moment. You'd like help speaking to her?"

Ricky threw up his hands. "Yes! Geezum crow. You're a

medium! Why else would I be here? Please help me talk to my mom!"

No wonder he and Ezra got on. They're very similar. I nodded. "Okay."

"She's on lunch now but—"

"Wait, *now?*"

He rolled his eyes. "Dude, she's not gonna let some strange man in her house. Work is the best place for this."

"Oh god." I sighed. "Security is gonna love seeing me again."

Ricky bounced on his heels. "Come on. I have things I want to say to her. and then I want to ask you about something."

"Oh?"

"Yeah. Okay, look, this is kind of out there, alright? But have you ever thought about having a ghost assistant? Like, an assistant who *is* a ghost and not like… someone who assists with them?"

Oh god.

ABOUT THE AUTHOR

Meredith Spies (they/them/theirs) is a queer, nonbinary author who lives far away and writes queer-centered stories with romance in them and queer romances with stories in them. They believe that pineapple goes on pizza, that there's no reason for open toed boots, and everyone deserves a happily ever after.

My Linktree: www.linktr.ee/meredithspies
Find my entire back list, new releases, upcoming releases ARC opportunities, social media and more!